THE
Children of Wicked Hallow

A Novel by

Leisel

The
Children of Wicked Hallow

by

Leisel

Copyright January 2013

Cover Art and Design by
Courtney Kurtenbach

ISBN-13: 978-0615791784
ISBN-10: 0615791786

Visit us on Leiselbooks.com to get all the information on our books.

Contents

The Children of Wicked Hallow

Chapter 1

I remember precisely the way it happened. The sin of pride, the sin of lust, wrath and envy-some I completely confess committing. The sin of lying-I don't know where that one goes, but that's a big one. It wasn't me who committed the lying, *that* was another. Truth, I wish I could tell you how important the truth was.

I loved mysteries, I loved solving the likes of *Sherlock Holmes.* And *Rebecca*, by Daphne de Maurier. I loved *Rebecca.* She knew about ghosts...about spirits that came and went. I would often go into that world of *Rebecca* , pretend I would be her, pretend that it was I who was walking the halls of Manderly. I was as shy as she, and I always wished that a rich wonderful man would someday want me as well. I

1

would read in the shade in my backyard oak for hours on end until the shadows of the evening would bring me indoors. Yes, *Rebecca* was my only constant companion. The backyard was the one place I felt like I belonged- that, and the public library. There's a reason reading became a top priority- reading was free. Once when I was in third grade I got the lead part in a school play, and I worked hard to get it right. I was little red riding hood, and the school provided costumes, or rather the teachers did, and when the day came for my portrayal I remember looking down into the audience where my teacher said was reserved for my family-they never showed up. I remember looking down at the seats and their emptiness mocked me for ever expecting them to be filled. I *knew* they would not be there, but I had *hoped.* The teacher, Miss Swearingen came up to me after the play was over and gave me a big hug, she knew I was disappointed and there began our relationship. I believe she knew how things were in my house, and she tried to make up for the lack of interest at home. She suggested that I spend more time in the library, because there were stacks of stories about children who eventually made good. My parents made it a point never to waste money on me, or time, I learned.

I wasn't always the unapologetic loser I portray-there was a time when I felt complete, when there was another half to my whole. He is the invisible companion that keeps me company and now he's only one of the ghosts that swirl around in my head. I was born a twin, with a cute, little cherub faced boy as my mate. I remember rolling on the floor in our diapers with Marcus, playing hide and seek and my mom singing the song, *'Ring around the Rosie'*, She was always with us then, *always*. I can see Marcus's angel face sticking up between the bars on the crib that we shared, waking me up from sleep on that dreadful night.   3

He was crying that night when my dad stormed into the room, whisked him up, yelling in Marcus' face, red from screaming-he shook him; There was a loud sound of a 'snap', I remember the sudden quiet – as if someone had turned off the light switch. I remember Marcus's limp body being held out by dad, and suddenly dad carrying him out with Marcus's silence. I heard my mom wailing, and Dad's cries as if he could not believe what he had done. But they never came back to our room, suddenly I was conspicuously alone. And that's all I can remember about Marcus. Then 12 months later Nancy was born, she was what you would call a 'replacement' child for my mom, but dad never held his tongue on another boy.

We never talked about Marcus after that, I didn't dare. It was if he had never existed. But I missed him, I knew him from the womb,and there was an empty space beside me where he should have been.

4

That's why I've always been the 'good' one, the one that never got into trouble. I was frightened that I would be next – that I would be taken away in the night, never to appear again – never missed. Marcus was my ghost, he was part of me that should have gone on living, and I missed him terribly.

My life is quickly becoming unraveled, they're talking about putting me in the general population, and that scares me more than the ghosts I swear I've always seen. And oh, the nightmares. Nancy visits me in my nightly visions like a mad succubus. When I don't dream about the illusions of Nancy I dream about *other* things. Dreadful things being done to me by a crazy man that has no face. I can't remember if these are 'dreams', or if they are things that actually happened. My psychologist tells me that my dreams are bound to be dis-conjoined, random like my childhood. I'm not so sure. I wake up sweating, my clothes drenched from my crazy man nightmares. I can't allow myself to think about him now; my life has been screwed up even without him.

My older sister, Jolene is the only visitor I've had throughout years, shes the only loyal person I know. Her last visit with me she told me that Dad had died. I wasn't sad. In fact I wasn't really feeling anything for the man. He was a smug, arrogant, insufferable braggart, who never spoke kindly of a another man in his whole life. I've heard that prejudice is learned, and if it is, he was one hell of a teacher. Perhaps that's why I feel like telling my side of the story-because his death brought it all back with a vengeance.

I guess that's why the incidents that took place way back are becoming so important to me now. I say 'incidents' because I don't want to make you turn away in horror that a young girl could do this brutal act, that

6

three people would be gone by summers end. One I missed, but the others-deserved it.

I was 14 that summer of '74, and my younger sister, Nancy who was 13; along with a pair of sisters, Carla and Cyndi Charbonneau who were roughly the same age who lived next door. The Charbonnneau girls had parents who's names also started with a 'C', Carolyn and Cass. They had the perfect family, it seemed to me, they spoke- not yelled to each other and hugged one another, they seemed to actually *express love* in their family. Although the name game was a bit sickening to me. Carla had in incurable case of the hiccups, it seemed and it had always had it's charm. But that was *before*. And then there was my cousin, Margo who was also 13. Nancy and Margo were thicker than thieves, going off by themselves, never telling me where. We had heard rumors of Margo's parents getting a divorce, and so she was staying with us for most of the summer of '74.

Now even before that summer I had been jealous of the two of them always going off and having secrets. I didn't have people around my own age, not that it would have made any difference; I didn't have friends, period. They had secret signs and tried to make a special language that only they knew, but I had cracked that language easily, I pretended *not* to understand so they would talk around me.

We lived in a lower middle class house in Denver, with neatly clipped yards and manicured hedges -it was long before I knew what lower middle class was. I personally loved the neighborhood, it was like living on an island in the Pacific, I'll tell you how- at the end of our block there was a steep ravine, though we always called it 'the gulley', or more sinister name is 'Wicked Hallow' as people began to call the gulley- a miniature Grand Canyon with railroad tracks running down the the floor of the canyon-you could hear the train whistle at 10 and 5 precisely. I loved to stand at the edge, looking into the valley below-you could almost see forever though the cut in the earth with trees lining the way-it was breathtaking! There was a creek that ran through the ravine in a lazy 'S' shape, making a bridge where it met the rickety railroad tracks, it wound around a block away coming up on the other end of the street-where it was made into a park. Like I said, a little island in the Pacific.

One summer day in 1974 when Margo's mom, my Aunt Paula, dropped her off they were off once more. In this lost world I had created, my jealousy would wind up again, and I tried to bypass those feelings by hanging out with my neighbors, Carla and Cyndi. But they made it clear that they wanted to hang out with Nancy and Margo, because they appeared to have a much better time than the outcast wretch I projected. So, I was rejected to be to one who hung out to the side, with the four of them passing secrets to one another, and sharing a united laugh against me.

I was determined that it wouldn't get me down, however, and I decided to take the long walk to the library where I felt completely at ease with myself. The library was a mile away, the opposite direction from the ravine. The way to the library passed the little emerald park on the other end of the block that always a treat for me. I had to pass over a bridge that went over the creek that wound around the blocks. I liked to stop on that bridge and gaze down watching the minnows swim, just as I had every summer. I enjoyed putting my fingers in the cool water, watching the fish swim round. I would stroll up and down the small hills that lay between me and the library. When I finally arrived at my destination, I would stay as long as I dared,   10 walking slowly between the long rows of books, losing myself until the time came for me to go home.

Having my Pee-Chee folder and newly discovered books, I would start back for the house feeling like I was having the *real* fun, and how Nancy and Margo and the Charbonneau girls would get themselves into trouble. I would hear them at night, Nancy took Marcus's space-we shared the same room, until they thought I was sleeping then they would talk in regular voices about how they liked the boy who lived in the duplex behind our house, and across the alley.

His name was Walter Couly, and they were so impressed that his name *made* him sound 'cool', as if he ever had anything to do with his name- I was repulsed! Walter was the one boy that I could not stand. He had made himself into the neighborhood bully, knocking balls out of kids hands, that were younger than he was, and to young too actually fight back. I had seen him when he was younger, when he used to go outside playing in dirty underwear, wearing no shoes. I had seen him playing with his excrement, delighted that he could play with it like silly putty-I felt sorry for him *once*-but I managed to bypass that feeling fast enough.

However, this was 1974 and he *did* disgust me. Nancy and Margo had whispered that they were going to meet up with him in the gully, and I was shocked that they would ever decide to do such a thing. I said so, to which they started laughing at me and told me to mind my own business. I could have said I was going to tell mom on them, but I also wanted them to accept me, so I remained silent.

The next morning they woke early, had a quick breakfast and were out on their adventure. I studied over my oatmeal and remained quiet about their whereabouts. I had a book with me, as I usually did, which my mom told me not to read at the table, so I put my book under the table and read when she wasn't looking.

"It's a nice day," mom said, "aren't you going out?"

"I'm going to read in the shade out back." I said.

That was my plan, only I didn't tell her that the other part of my day was going to be spying on Nancy and Margo. I walked out the back door and made my way to the shady part of the oak, laying a blanket down and making sure mom saw me there. Then she was off to do her laundry, and I was off through the back gate and down the alley careful not to make any noise. The alley dropped off into the ravine and I was nervous because I didn't see any trace of them.

I knew they couldn't be at Walter's duplex, for his mother was a drunk and often spent her days in comatose sleep. I had seen her beat Walter when he disturbed her, so I was confident they were not there.

The only place where they could have gone was into the hallow, so I continued there. I took a long look around the top and didn't see them, so I ventured down, very carefully down the long steep hill.

I didn't worry about dirtying my clothes. They were play clothes that my mother made me wear as to keep my nice clothes clean. Funny I didn't even have any 'nice' clothes, and equally as funny mom didn't have a problem buying my older sister, Jolene, new clothes or for that fact buying new clothes for Nancy. I was made to stand alone, the middle sister who was made to suffer this embarrassment.

Jolene was 3 years my senior, which in teenage years was an eternity. Jolene always had her record albums of the Beatles and Elvis playing, and her friends who talked endlessly of boys-a passion we did not share. She always looked fashionable enough, but I looked a bit strange with the same clothes folded up at the cuffs and again at the legs, I must have looked like a rag doll. I didn't have a stereo of my own so I liked laying on the cool wood floor outside Jolene's bedroom, as we did not have air conditioning, listening to the music they played with the door closed.

So now I was going off in search of Nancy, Margo and Walter, feeling like a spy. In fact, that was the game I played- I was a spy on a mission and finding them was my objective-but I had to do it quietly and without their notice. I reached the bottom of the hill where the creek and railroad tracks met, and I walked along the bank.

Suddenly I heard voices, that of Margo and then Walter. Finally I heard Nancy's voice, there was no mistaking her high-pitched laugh. The voices were coming from the bridge under the railroad tracks. I decided to hide myself behind one of the tall bushes that grew dense in the summer. Now I could hear what was said.

"Come on, Walter," it was Margo's voice, "tell us, which one of us do you like better?"

"I like you both, you're both very cute- you know- for girls."

Then I heard them squeal with laughter. They continued.

"Walter, you must think one of us is prettier-come on- which one?"

"I don't want to hurt no one's feelings. If I say I like one of you more, then the other one's feelings are hurt. I don't wanna say."

"Walter," Margo prodded, "go on, you say which one of us, and I promise you that we're both cool."

"Okay." Walter said like they were prying his teeth, "I like Nancy better."

"See?" Margo said, "You didn't hurt feelings here. Now that we know that, we can continue."

I could hear Nancy and Margo's whispering, then they said, "Margo says she has to go get a watch for us to use, don't you Margo?" a giggling Nancy said.

"Yeah. I'll be back in 20 minutes- did you hear that Walter? I'll be back in 20, so you two can be together-alone."

"Huh?" a dimwitted Walter said as if he didn't get it.

"Explain it to him, Nancy. I'll be back *later.*"

Margo was now giggling as she ran out of the tunnel, right past where I was hiding. She scrambled up the hill, kicking up dust as she ran. I suddenly felt the embarrassment of being in a place where I could not explain myself, a hot flush came over my face and I started to sneak away, leaving Nancy and Walter doing who knows what under the darkness of the tunnel.

17

I slowly started walking two blocks away, where Perry street carved it's way through the ravine. I wandered about, continuing the game where I was a spy, jumping behind trees until I reached a huge park a mile away, opposite the way to the library. There I came to Sloane's lake and I could see fisherman on the shores, unaware that I was watching them. A weedy smell came out of the lake, but it was pleasant all the same. The men were here now, working on the lawn leaving the area with a freshly mowed scent. I took my time and walked around the lake, stopping at the swings and playing with the little kids. The lake looked like the blue of the sky. Reflected in the sky I could see the outline of the mountains, with the white capped peaks in the distance.

I took off my shoes and started running my toes through the grass, it felt so warm and sensuous. I was in the shade of the tall cherry tree where a bee was droning

18

about a blossom. But there was the hint of a breeze that kept my ragged hair in my face, I kept on pulling my hair behind my ears. I decided it was time to take the long walk home when it I suddenly remembered that I forgot to ask my mother for permission to go- I know I was 14, but my parents were sticklers about things like this. I began to run, panting until I thought my lungs would burst. I suddenly heard the cawing of a crow, leaving me with a strange feeling of foreboding.

When I was within two blocks I had my first warning as to what was happening and I wondered why I could hear sirens; I wondered where the fire was burning. Coming closer I realized with dread it's tragic sense, and with every step it became more real. My mother had called the police and there was yellow tape blocking off the area to the ravine. I thought it was meant for me, but it wasn't. Red lights were going off like flares, the cherry

19

-red tops of the police cars were flashing everywhere. Mom had seen me through the chaos and ran towards me, grabbing me by the shoulders and shouting,

"Where have you been? I thought you were going to be out back, reading a book?"

"I went for a walk, mom. Really. What's happening? Tell me, what's going on?" I was frantic, but not as frantic as mom, she had the look of a person who's been dreadfully crying.

"It's Nancy!" she sobbed, "Margo came home about half an hour ago, and she was screaming someone did this to her. I followed her down to the tunnel under the tracks- and it was awful! Who could do this to my little girl?"

"What did they do? TELL ME!"

"She's dead!" mom screamed, "someone killed her, they murdered my little girl!"

Chapter 2

I felt as though I had been kicked in the gut, the air gone from my body. I looked over at Margo, she was sitting on the couch, with a policeman talking to her. She was in pain, she looked like she had been crying, but what she said wasn't making sense to me.

"We were playing a game. She was hiding from me and I was supposed to find her-kind of a hide and seek game." Margo cried.

"So you have no idea who might have done this? No idea at all?" the policeman asked.

"No, I have no idea." she lied.

My brain spinned off in a panic-*she has no idea who did this? Why hasn't she named Walter as the one who was the last person to see Nancy alive?*

"You liar!" I yelled at Margo, "You have an idea, in fact you know who did this to Nancy!"

She jumped up and flew at me, punching me and tearing at my eyes. I punched back, not wanting to hurt her, but she was acting like she wanted to kill me. The policeman quickly tore us apart and Margo said,

"You don't know anything, you filthy pig."she was seething, with her teeth clenched and slobber forming in the corners of her mouth.

"I knew the two of you were going to a meeting at the tunnels."

"Liar!" Margo didn't look like she was going to tell what she knew.

"Hold on," the policeman said, "tell us about this meeting." he was looking at Margo, then at me.

"She doesn't know anything, she's trying to get attention." Margo looked at me with those eyes of hers, grey and narrow.

"Okay. That's enough!" the cop demanded, "Get these

two in different rooms right now! Come on, take her." he called to the other officers who promptly took me into the kitchen.

"Now tell me what you know. It will go help us if you cooperate." he sat down next to me, as if he were my friend. "They were going to a meeting this morning? How would you know this?"

I stalled. "I may have misspoken. I don't know what plans they had. I'm in shock-my little sister is dead." but I wasn't in shock, I wasn't feeling anything yet.

"Come on," he said, "tell me what you know." and he said it in a way that made me think he suspected me. His eyes were going up and down my body as if he were looking for scratches or blood.

But I was clean, I didn't have a scratch on me. I didn't have anything to do with my sister's murder.

"How did she die?" I asked him, with a reality hitting me that she really was gone. I deadpanned a look at him, and then the other officer with the knowledge that I did *not* know.

"Her throat was ripped, from ear to ear." he whispered, but he still said it loud enough so that my mom heard as she started to wail.

"I'm not a suspect, am I?" I innocently asked.

"No, I don't think so...it looks like it was done by a strong man. Whomever it was would be covered in blood." he said that quieter this time. "But I need to record your full statement for the record. Now where have you been for the last hour?" he took out a pad of paper and pen and started writing down what I said.

When they were finally done talking with all of us, they packed up inside the house, then finished down at the tunnel with the coroner, leaving so much yellow tape you would have thought it was a parade. I found out later that they had taken blood and tissue samples, along with about a hundred pictures from every angle. I'll never forget how my sister's body looked, tucked away in the little white body bag, stained with blood, as they drove away.

Mother had to have a doctor come in and give her a sedative. Dad finally rushed into the house as one policeman was obviously waiting for him to arrive.

"What's happened to my little girl?" he screamed as the coroner's car was driving away. I heard the policeman take him outside and tell him what had gone on. I could hear what I never thought I would hear again-my dad was breaking down. The neighbors were outside now, some of them coming over to Dad, trying to give him comfort. I noticed the girls, Carla and Cyndi come out of their house, joining up with Margo. They were in secret conference, making it clear I wasn't invited. I tried to join them, but was rebuffed by Margo.

"Why don't you get away from us, *liar!"* Margo yelled.

I tried to convince her otherwise. "I didn't tell the police anything useful. I kept quiet." I pleaded.

"Why? I expected you to crumble. You're a tattletale, anyway." Margo smirked and turned away.

"You didn't tell on Walter. Why not?" I asked.

"Because Walter wasn't with her when she died. He was no where near the tunnel." Margo acted tough.

"How could you know that? You were in the alley coming up from the ravine- I know because I saw you."

"Thank you." Margo said with insolence.

"I think you're the liar. I think you know who did this, and I'm going to tell the police- you can be sure of that."

I was trying to get her to spill her guts, but I saw her put on her shield of armor, she wasn't going to crack.

The Charbonneau girls suddenly joined in, "We were at

26

a swim meet at the Y, we were so surprised to come home and find all this." Carla said through her hiccups with Cyndi shaking her head as if to say the exact same thing. "Do tell us, what happened?"

Margo turned her back and got in the middle between the neighbors and me.

"Nancy and I were going to meet a boy down at the tunnel this morning," Margo started, "then he didn't show and I went back to the house because I forgot to take these pebbles to mark our path with- and when I returned she was lying there, in a pool of blood. I ran back to the house screaming for Auntie to come with me. Something terrible had happened!"

'OH, you awful liar!' I thought. That's not what happened at all. Why was she shielding Walter? I wanted to join in their conversation and tell them the truth, but I did not. I decided not to tell anyone

27

about Walter. At least until I could sort this out. Walter hasn't been innocent since the day he was born. Slowly my suspicions started. Growing like the Kudzu weeds, strangling the beautiful plants it was unfortunate enough to come across. But at least I knew that Aunt Paula would be picking up Margo from us tonight. After all, what's worse, divorce or death?

Chapter 3

A strange quiet descended over the household, and we all tiptoed around those first days, at least until mother could go without her sedatives. It was on one of those lazy days of summer when we started to plan my sister's funeral- it was to be held on Saturday. While lying on the wooden floor listening to Jolene and her friend, Vicky, listening to *Jim Croce*, when I heard her talk for the first time since Nancy's death.

"I know I should wear black," Jolene said, "but what would you think if I wore a white scarf? Too much?" Jolene said. She was talking about Nancy's funeral.

"Naw, it looks groovy." Vicky responded.

"I don't know what to do or say to Mom and Dad. I try to stay out of their way, what would you do?"

"Don't know. I've never had a sister, let alone having one that's been murdered. Weird stuff." Vicky said.

"Tell me about it." Jolene said under her breath.

"Do the police have any clues to who might have done it?" Vicky asked.

"I think they're in the dark about this as much as anyone." she stopped, "But you know, I think that Margo knows more than she's telling."

"Go ahead, tell me!" Vicky said dripping with morbid curiosity.

"Yeah, I mean if you could have heard her that day-she sounded like she had information that she didn't want to share. I think she's hiding a very important clue."

"Maybe you should get her alone, you know-ask her about it. Maybe she is hiding something-you never know." Vicky sounded convinced. She always sounded like an expert and her word was final.

"Margo is a little bitch, pardon my French. She's so slimy, she leaves a trail."Jolene sounded sour.

30

I rolled away from my place on the floor and went to my room. I guessed it was *my* room now that Nancy was gone. My mom hadn't the nerve to enter the room now that she was dead. I closed the door and laid my head on my pillow. Things had changed so much in such a short time, I hadn't time to mourn Nancy. I turned my head into my pillow and started to cry.

………..…………………………………………………………………

Before I knew it, it was time for Nancy's funeral. People looked serious enough, some resembled my parents, my aunts and uncles. They looked desperate and tearful, some of them cried at the funeral making dark circles under their eyes. I was dressed in black, my folks didn't have the money to buy me a new dress, so the

31

Charbonneaus bought me a plain black jumper from Goodwill.

The funeral was taking place in the graveyard, in an area known as 'Little Angels'. It was where the babies and young children were buried. I could see the hole in the ground, dug especially for Nancy. Right next to Marcus' headstone, she would sleep right next to him -I was jealous of this-that was supposed to be reserved for me. But now Nancy would get this, too. Then I realized that Nancy would get *my plot- it's like she was taking my place-I would get the chance to live while she got the chance to die.* Then I crossed myself, my fingers moving over my body in a old bucolic ritual, thanking the stars that I had another chance.

I saw Margo across the fields, her family upfront and very visible. Later when it was time for people to walk by and tell my parents how sorry they were but she was uncharacteristically quiet. Aunt Paula was giving her brother, my dad, hugs and was squeezing him when she said in her loud voice, "I feel so bad that my little Margo was the last one to see your Nancy alive!"

My dad straightened up his spine and froze. My mom started with a new flood of tears. Aunt Paula turned to my Dad and said, "Oh, I'm sorry. Have I said something?"

Mom ran off to the bathroom and I followed.

"Don't pay attention to Aunt Paula, she doesn't know what's she's saying." I said comfortingly.

"I know she doesn't." mom said patting my arm, "It's just her way."

I put my arms around her neck and gave her a big hug, but she was definitely *not* hugging back. So I said the unthinkable.

"I love you, Mom." she was totally silent, and stared at me with vacant eyes. It was at that moment that I knew what I had always suspected; she didn't love me, that it had stopped with Marcus. I gave up.

Right after they lowered Nancy's coffin into the ground, I saw Margo again and I motioned for her to meet me behind the large floral piece made of roses, and surprisingly, she agreed.

"What's so important?" she asked.

"Margo," I began, "I know that you had a meeting with Walter on the day my sister died. Why are you protecting him?"

"And how, exactly, would you know that?"

"I heard the two of you talking the night before. I was awake- I was only pretending to sleep."

"So?"

"Come on! You're deliberately covering for him and I want to know why!"

She turned away from me, and I called out after her. "I

34

think you should go to the police and tell them that you met with him. They probably need to talk to him, at least to get his side of the story."

"I think you shouldn't talk about this." she turned towards me once again.

"What if I told them that I knew for sure that Walter was there?"

"Accidents happen," she started to walk away, crushing the petals of a pale pink rose between her fingers, "just saying."

"What was that? Are you trying to scare me?"

"Aren't you scared?" she said narrowing those eyes at me.

"No, I'm not. I've never been scared of *you.*" I postured with my back straight.

"I would reconsider." she said as she walked away firmly crushing the remains of the rose beneath her feet.

Chapter 4

I slept in fits that night, having dreams about
Nancy's funeral. I couldn't get restful sleep to escape my
anxiety, it was taking a toll on me. My hair was starting to
fall out in clumps. I dreamt about how Nancy was the
favorite child, the baby. I could hear sobs coming from
the vents-it was Mom. Even though my parents bedroom
was in the basement, I could hear their voices rise up, it
was like talking on a loudspeaker. I covered my ears with
my pillow and rolled to one side.

I heard it. I know I did. I heard an unfamiliar
crunching sound from outside my window! Then I peeked
over and I saw a shadow that made my hair stand on end.
It was a man's shadow, and he was moving about as if he
were looking for a way to open my window. I opened my
mouth to scream, but nothing came out. I couldn't move

at all, not even if he had come crashing through the window.

I've never known fear such as this before. I thought he was there to frighten me, and it worked. I don't know where my strength came from, but I remember jumping up and turning on my light. The illumination must have scared him, because he was suddenly gone. I ran to Jolene's room and jumped into bed with her, waking her up.

"What the hell?" Jolene said while trying to kick me out of her queen sized bed.

"There was a man at my window. There was a man..." I stuttered.

"Oh my god. You've been talking to the neighbors, haven't you?" Jolene asked.

"No, I haven't. Why?"

"Just because the police are saying that there might be

a madman in the neighborhood doesn't mean it's true."
she said to calm me.

"What are you talking about?" I screamed. This was
news to me. "Can't I sleep with you tonight?"

"NO! I'm trying to sleep, you'll keep me up."

"Please, *please.*" I begged her. She looked at me
sighing dejectedly, dropping her head.

"Ohhhh, alright. But keep still, don't jump around." she
said as she went to turn out the light.

"Nooooo!!" I shrieked once more, "Please,
please...with the light on!"

"Good god!" she said with a finality that I did not want
to test. She did, however, leave the light on.

…..

The following morning I shuffled into the kitchen to

have breakfast. I hardly slept at all and I was a sorry sight with my tangled hair and unkempt pajamas. Jolene was up stirring the oatmeal.

"Mom had a rough night. She's sleeping in." Jolene said.

"K." I said.

"Why don't you take your book outside today? It's supposed to be a sunny day." Jolene said trying to sound cheerful.

"I don't know about that." I was still terrified from the night before.

"Don't be a coward! Go outside and read. I'll be right here if you need me. Go on."

So I finished the unappealing oatmeal and took my favorite volume of Sherlock Holmes to the shade of the oak tree in the backyard. I spread out my blanket and went through the motions of reading, but I just could not concentrate. My eyes wandered over to the back gate and I saw what stood my hair for a second time in 12 hours: the chain link fence was open! I walked over as if I were walking on hot coals, slowly, tenderly-and had a look. It was not the kind of lock that you could undo easily. There were footprints that belonged to a person who was running in a hurry. I looked at Walter's dilapidated duplex and saw him staring through the window. I was more than scared, I was panicked. I tried to hide myself behind the huge lilac bushes that ran behind our house along the back gate. Then I crept over to my bedroom window, the one that looked over the yard, and I saw proof that someone had tried to pry up my window. A screwdriver was on the ground and you could see pry marks on the window lock.

Who had been there last night? Walter or the madman I heard about?Should I tell the police? I knew that I couldn't tell my mother or father of what I found, I thought about telling Jolene.

In the 70's we were forced to do Civil Defense drills once a month in case of a nuclear attack, and I'll be honest, they used to scare me to my core. The chilling sound of the CD siren becoming louder and stronger, my heart would catch in my throat-I often had visions of seeing bombs falling from the sky and the last thing I would ever see-the bright light that's set off by the bombs hitting the Earth within the mushroom shaped cloud. The duck and cover drills that they would have us do in school were useless, so what, would there be a nuclear attack that would lay barren waste land for miles but somehow we would be safe under our desks? No, I know now that we would have all been ashes if there was an attack. But they made us *feel better.* This was an incident that scared me in a new way, a personal way, where I wasn't part of decent society, waving flags and saying the Pledge of Allegiance. I was on my own.   42

Chapter 5

That weekend I heard them fighting in the basement. My mom was being defensive and accused my dad of being responsible for Nancy's death as well as for Marcus- I heard the sound of my mom being slapped, then I heard her sobs-she was crying. And who could blame her? For when my dad was drunk, as he was now, he became an angry drunk. The sounds of smacks and Mom's cries went on as they usually did. I did not know how my Mom could stay with a man who beat her so. Perhaps she stayed for us, for the kids. Maybe she was a sadistic perv who enjoyed the beatings- I have no idea of what kind of relationship they had, and I didn't want to find out now.

Dad had finally pushed his liver to the edge and had the beginnings of dementia. Mom used to have a light in her eyes, but that went out on that summer day when Nancy was murdered. She has never been the same since, she used to have a twinkle in her eyes when she spoke, but that was gone. I don't think I ever saw her laugh again.

Most of the time I stayed in my room under the covers until it was peaceful again, other times when it was warm I would go outside and imagined I was someone else entirely. That's what I loved about summertime in Denver- there were always places to go when you had to get away. So I made my way out to the oak tree again and tried to block out the sounds of their fighting by immersing myself into one of my favorite novels.

But I could not block out the sounds that day. I decided to take a peek across the back alley and see if I could deduce anything about Walter. I crept up to the chain link fence, hiding behind the tall lilac bushes and tried to see if there was any activity. I could hear voices, young male voices. I determined that it was Walter and his cronies. I heard one of them, Peter boy and another named Nick,

44

however I remembered when in first grade the teacher called out his legal name, 'Leslie'- to which he turned a bright red. He asked her if she could call him 'Nick', but the damage was done- all the kids teased him about his name until he turned into a bully, like the rest. They sounded as if they were trying to keep their voices down, but there was only an alley between us.

Nick spoke first, "I don't know Walt, I would keep it quiet if I were in your shoes. No need in stirring up a hornet's nest, ya know?"

Peter boy was eating a doughnut, adding to his paunch as usual and added, "But just between us, how was she? Pretty good, eh?"

Walter was quiet for a moment, I think I moved and stepped on a rock which made a noise. Walter must have heard, then said, "Let's go to the gully and talk, being here gives me the creeps. You never know if her snoop sister is

45

around."

The three of them walked down the alley and I couldn't hear them anymore. What was Walter doing? Was he giving his buddies a lowdown on how my sister was before he attacked and killed her? I was so angry with him at that moment, angry with parents and angry the world. So, I decided I would go the library, after all nobody would notice my being gone and perhaps I could blow off some steam.

I walked across the front yard and across the park towards the library. It was noon and I didn't notice clouds gathering in the west. I was a block from the library when it began raining sheets. I ran for the door and sat down soaking wet. The librarian came over to me and said,

"Looks like you just made it. Here, you look like you could use this." and held out a towel. I gratefully took it and started drying off my head.

"Thank you." I said. "are you sure it's okay?"

She looked at me curiously, then she suddenly realized who I was and said,

"Yes." she said, "You're the one, right?"

"The one?" I was perplexed.

"The one who recently lost her sister. I'm so sorry." she said it as though she weren't sorry at all-just curious.

"Oh, yes. Thanks." I said without knowing what she was sorry for. Then it hit me. I guess this was a huge story and I was square in the middle. I thought about it and saw her walk back to her desk, then I decided to ask.

"Do you have any newspapers I could read, about my sister, I mean?"

"Are you sure, honey? I don't want to give you nightmares. That's rough stuff they've written, stories about your family." she looked like she was concerned, but I told her,

47

"I'm sure. My folks won't mind, it's just that we don't get the paper."

She made her customary forehead crease, then told me,

"Okay, honey. I'll get them for you." she walked to the backroom and brought out a stack of papers about a foot tall.

"You can look it up in all these papers, but keep them in order, I haven't cataloged them yet." she dropped them in front of me and I thanked her.

I carried the load of papers to a back table where no one could see me. I was speechless! The events that took place were unrecognizable to me, the reporters were simply making up stuff to sell their papers. I was surprised that they didn't find a way to use Bigfoot in the stories.

I carefully put them back in order and laid my damp head down, using the papers as a pillow. I thought, *'Wow.*

I didn't even know that the police were looking at my dad as a suspect. He didn't have an alibi for when my sister was killed, so they questioned him as well. The other paper says it's a crazy man from the asylum. What asylum are they even talking about?'

I decided to ask the nice librarian. I chugged the papers over to her desk and politely put them down.

"Are you done?" she asked.

"Yes, thank you." I stalled, mustering up the courage, "I was wondering if you could tell me any *other* information?" I smiled at her with a playful grin.

"Like what, dear?"

"In the papers they spoke of an asylum. Do you know where this asylum is located? I've never even heard of it."

"Oh dear!" she looked like she had spilled a gigantic secret. "You don't know about the mental asylum? It closed about a year ago, and that's all I can say."

49

"Closed? I mean I never heard about it when it was open." I said it so loud that I must have tripped the alarm on her librarian mode. She immediately put her hand on my shoulder and told me to keep my voice down. She took me to the back of the library, I don't know why, surely I was the only other person there. Once in the back she started telling me in a whisper.

"Yes, there was a mental asylum not far from where you live."

"You know where I live?" I stupidly asked her.

"Of course I do. You *do* have a library card that shows your address, besides the papers practically showed your house, and I know that's only about a mile from here. Certainly I know." she put in this last because I must have looked like a frightened puppy. Then she went on, "It's west of your house, on the other side of Sheridan. There had been a lot of arguments back and forth about funding for an asylum right in the city limits. Well, last year the committee that wanted it gone finally got their way when a budget crisis called for it to close."

"Where did they put the people who were living there?" I asked.

"That's the thing, isn't it? They didn't have anywhere to put them. They let them right on the streets. You might have noticed some of them hanging out on Colfax, they look like bums and such, but some say they live in the tunnels that run throughout the city. You shouldn't go down there if you value your life!" she said.

"Surely they can't just put people back on the street like that, can they?"

"They can and they did. I've had quite the time keeping them from using this library as a refuge. I certainly don't want trash like *that* using our restrooms and hanging out here   51 pretending to read. Not here, not on my watch."

"What was the name of this asylum?"

"Heilstratten Asylum for the Criminally Insane. Although I've heard it called *Hell-stratten.*" she continued to speak in quiet volumes.

I was shocked! Why have I never heard of this place for the wickedly insane? I asked her quickly before this island where we were the only two souls, vanished.

"Do you have any books on this Heilstratten?"

"Yes, as a matter of fact we do. There's only one. However, it's a reference book so it can't leave the library." she walked over to the reference section and pulled it out, she knew exactly where to find it.

"Thanks." I muttered and took the large hardcover book to the back table again and began my education on *Hell-stratten.*

I remembered when it stopped raining that I had not

asked for permission, again to leave. I started walking

back home after I gave the librarian a cursory nod and

didn't say a word. Which was wise, because she looked

like she didn't know me since there were now two other

people in the library. I walked along the sidewalk

stepping in puddles as I went along getting my shoes wet,

but I thought my mom wouldn't say a word when she saw

them- and it turned out I was right. It was late afternoon

now, and the sun was in position in the west to go down

for the day.

I saw Carla and Cyndi playing tag in their front yard

when I walked up to them. Carla, the older of the two, was

always trying to be a fashion plate, and right now she had

on a new, red pantsuit with platform shoes that were made

of clear acrylic and fake fish swimming inside. I suppose

she was trying to channel *Maude,* from television.

"Hi guys," I said. They stopped running and came

over to me.

"Where h-have you been?" Carla asked through her usual hiccups.

"Your mother was mad when she came out looking for you." Cyndi said.

"Ummm." I said, "I don't want to go inside. Can I come over to your house?"

Their response was the usual 'no', but then they must have felt sorry for me and suddenly said that it was okay. We walked up into their Jack and Jill bedroom on the second floor, facing the backyard and started talking.

"Are you s-scared?" Carla hiccuped.

"You mean because they haven't caught the man who killed Nancy?" I shrugged.

"I would be scared. I think you would be, too." Cyndi said.

I moved towards Carla's back window and pulled her

blue print curtains to one side and did a general overview of the neighborhood from the back. I looked one way towards the avenue and it was eerily deserted. I turned my head to see where the alley gave into the gully where two teenagers stood kissing. I looked beyond where they were, steep into the green ravine, again I saw nothing.

Then a small movement brought my eyes back to Walter's duplex. Someone had been looking out of his back window, I'm positive. I saw the curtain moving back and forth as if I had just missed him. Why was he watching my house?

Voices of Carla and Cyndi brought me back.

"Do you want to play a g-game?" Carla asked, "We have all kinds here- there's the Dreamy Date- h-hey, we even have a *Ouija* board!" she was very excited about this as she pulled it out.

"Carla," Cyndi said, "You know we're supposed to get

Mom's permission before we start playing that one! Put it back, she's at work."

"Okay." Carla said, "I guess we can play the dating one," she started giggling. "Let's play with the *Ouija* board on the s-sly-what do you say, Cyndi?"

Carla got a devilish look in her eye. They both started to laugh.

"I'll lock the door so if Mom comes home early she won't know what we've done!"

"Okay, now make a circle around the board, one or two people can play, let's do two. Easy peazy!" Carla told me, "put your fingers on the palette, and I'll put mine on the other side-there!" she was so excited she could hardly keep still.

"What do we do next, Carla?" I asked.

"We're supposed to ask to talk to a d-dead person, so do you know any de-" she stopped and flushed as if a giant hand had slapped her.

Of course I knew a dead person! So did she, we all did. It became still, as if a wind had swept over a graveyard. We kept our fingers on the pallet on the board when it started moving. No one said a thing, and we looked at each other in amazement. The pallet started to spell a work that started with 'M', then it moved to 'U', then to 'R'.

I whispered, "What's happening? Are you moving it?"

Carla looked at me, she shook her head as we continued to watch the pallet slide across the board. The next letter was 'D', then 'E' and before it could spell the last letter, I pulled my fingers off the board as if they had been burned by a match. I pushed the board away from me in terror, and I shot up.

"Where are you going?" Cyndi asked me.

"You're kidding, right?" I said, "I'm going home."

"It's a game. It doesn't mean anything, right Carla?"

Carla had her fingers tucked away under her arms, still shaking her head.

"Let her go." Carla softly said, "I d-don't think we should have done that, play with the board."

"Oh, man!" Cyndi protested, "Don't tell me you're afraid that we've opened the door to hell? You're not, right?"

"It wasn't your fingers on the board! It got hot right towards the end, right when it tried to spelled *'murder'!*"

I shouted, "Maybe we did open a port hole to hell- I don't know, and I'm not going to stick around and find out!"

I tried to open the door, but it would not open. I yanked and pulled but it would not be budged!

"You have to unlock it first." Carla said rising from the floor. She came over and I protested, "I *did* unlock it!"

"Hmmm. You did." Carla mumbled.

Suddenly the whole door started to shake and we both took a step back. The door became bigger as if it had lungs and it was trying to take a deep breath.

"It's an earthquake!" Cyndi shouted.

"Then why is contained in the door, *alone?*" I asked.

Then, just as it started, it stopped and the door flew open as if on it's own accord. I ran out of there practically falling down the stairs. I couldn't get out of there fast enough.

Chapter 6

Later I kept quiet about the things that had happened-
no one would care, they had their own problems. We were
all silent at dinner time, a time that my mother usually
kept for family talk. But we weren't a family anymore.
You could see her fresh bruises, you could still see it in
her eyes, the loss.

Finally she asked me, "Where were you earlier? I
asked around and no one had seen you."

I kept my head down, "I walked to the library, no big
deal."

Mom's face turned red, then she started to yell, "It *is* a
big deal! I want you to stay around this house young lady,
not traipsing off to who knows where!"

I knew that her screaming at me would come-she was
still fighting with my father, only it was through me.

"But I..."

"Your mothers right!" Dad chimed in. This was not the usual way he dealt with arguments. "I think you should stay near home at all times, do you hear me?"

I looked pleadingly at Jolene. She shrugged her shoulders. "Just for awhile, till we know...just till we know."

I stewed over my dinner, I wasn't hungry after that, my stomach was twisting into knots. She had made canned mixed vegetables that were cold as ice, and when I tried to eat it, it tasted like metal. Then Mom added, "Finish you dinner, Missy! You don't get up from your seat till your dinner is completely gone."

It was a stalemate. I sat there playing with my food, making little mountains with my mashed potatoes and pushing the vegetables around my plate till 10:00 when she came into the kitchen and told me with her dead eyes,

"Go to bed."

I got up from my seat, still angry and pushed the food into the garbage, rinsed my plate then ran to my bedroom I laid in bed, tears coming down and I didn't know why when I heard a rustle in the leaves outside my window. I froze. I knew it was completely dark in my bedroom and the door was closed so there was no way whoever it was could see me. So I crept up to the corner of the window, trying to catch a glimpse of who the perpetrator was. I blinked, I saw a shadow and it was not moving, it just stood there looking in. The hairs on my neck were standing at attention once again.

Jolene came out of the bathroom and the light came underneath my door, and the shadow must have caught a glimpse, and he was off, running across the yard and over the fence. The dogs in the neighborhood started to bark and I ran into the hall and into Jolene's arms.

"What's up, squirt?" she asked me.

"Jo, I saw him at my window again!" my tears flowing full blast.

"Who? Who did you see?"

"I don't know, it was dark."

"Oh." she said as if she had figured it out, "Your scared because they haven't caught the person who killed Nancy yet, right?"

"No, no, no..." I pleaded, "that's not right! I *did* hear a man at my window and I swear you're not right!" I looked up at Jolene's face, it looked so old and weathered for seventeen. "Can I sleep with you tonight?"

Jolene groaned, then said, "Come on, one more night. But that's it, no more after tonight, got it?"

She grabbed my hand and took me to her bed where we started to talk, for the first time ever we spoke sister to sister.

"Jolene?"

63

"Yes."

"Did you know about the mental asylum that closed last year? The one that's only a mile from here?" I asked.

"Yeah, sure. We learned about it in school. I took a psychology class, we learned about it then."

"Why was it there, I mean so close."

"It opened over a century ago when this area was all wilderness. The city grew up around the asylum, not the other way around.

"Oh." I said, "And they called it *Hell*-stratten, I mean Heilstratten?"

"I've heard it both ways, actually. Heilstratten was it's formal name, but anyone who worked there or worse yet, came out of there called it Hell-stratten. I think that when they were sent to Heilstratten that it was a death sentence."

"What did they do to them?" I asked.

"The patients? I'm not exactly sure. They beat them with whips, they tied them down to their beds or shackled them to the walls. I've heard that there was no money towards the end, so they wouldn't even buy patients clothes. When the uniforms they were assigned to wore out, then they would go naked. There was no heat in the rooms because they, the doctors, mistakenly believed that the insane couldn't feel warmth or cold. It was merciless. There were dark times there, yes sir." Jolene said with a large yawn, then she said, "Goodnight." and that was all.

I stared at the ceiling for what seemed forever, till my dreams floated me away.

Chapter 7

The next morning was Saturday, which didn't mean much now that it was summer, we had all the time in the world. That was until my mom announced that *I* would be going to vacation Bible school. I pleaded that I did not want to go, and if I did why didn't Jolene have to go with me? My mother turned deaf ears to my plea's and told me once and for all that I could use some of the good things that were being taught at the Bible school, Heaven help me!

As it turned out going to Bible school wasn't such a terrible thing, The Conservative Baptist Church was on the next block over, so I did not have to wake up early to attend. It was four days a week, 9 to 12-not bad when you think all you had to do was listen to the youth pastor, Bill, testify and a do few worksheets.

But I savored my Saturday, when all I had to do was read my favorite novel, *Rebecca*, under the oak in the backyard. I put out my trusty blanket under the tree and had my variety of strong cheddar cheese cut into chunks with onion on savory crackers, flipped the pages to where I was last-the part where the girl was thinking about Rebecca; what she ate, who she wrote letters to...it was fascinating! The girl was scared of Mrs. Danvers, she didn't know why she frightened her so. She knew that Mrs. Danvers had adored the dead Rebecca, and was ashamed that she could not bring the glamour to Manderly as the perfect Rebecca had done. Oh, how I envied her, even with a character as wicked as a Mrs. Danvers, I could imagine myself living in that beautiful mansion by the sea, surrounded by the rose garden and practically smell the lush azalea happy valley. Even though technically *Rebecca* couldn't be called a 'ghost' story-it was still my favorite.

Then I looked over at Jolene who was making her way onto the chaise lounge chair where she could put on her music and listen to the music coming from her open bedroom window, tanning as she read her teen magazines. I found it slightly irritating that I could hear her music, because I loved the silence that usually accompanied me while I read. But I didn't want to start fighting with Jolene since she had let me sleep in her room two nights in a row. Instead I nodded at her and she nodded back. She yelled over to me, "Can you put some tanning lotion on my back?" to which I said with a heavy sigh, "Yeah, sure."

"You could read some of my magazines, if you want."

I found this unusual, for she never offered to let me read one of her style magazines before. I felt honored that she was including me, finally.

"Vicky is coming over in a bit, but if you pull that plastic chair over here, we could share them."

"Oh, okay!" I was thrilled with the attention she was showing me. Was she being sympathetic to me because my mom had told her to?

"Jolene?"

"Yeah?"

I asked her straight out, "Are you being nice to me because mom told you to?"

"Yes." she answered back at me. No excuses, no explanations, she was honest at least.

"Well then..." I was going to be honest with her, as well, "I think I'm going to read my book, then. Are you okay with that?"

"Yes." she said it again as she covered herself with eye shields and shifted her way to a comfortable position.

I wandered back to the shade of the oak tree and made

myself comfortable and continued my reading. Ants had found their way onto my platter of cheese and I grimaced, now I couldn't eat them at all, and I hated wasting that much good food.

I was thoroughly into my mystery when I saw a small black figure in the corner of my eye. I looked quickly, and it was gone. Had there been someone watching me? I went back to reading when I heard footsteps coming from the alley; this time I got up quickly and ran to the safety of the cover of the lilac bushes and listened. I listened very hard, there was definitely some movement coming from the other side of the bushes. I spread the lilac blossoms with my finger, just enough to see Walter and his friends gathered and talking in hushed tones. I couldn't hear clearly, but I thought I heard the words 'asylum' and 'lunatic'. Then I thought I saw Walter look straight at me-I froze. Then he looked away, I was so relieved. I saw his pals knocking his shoulders I heard, "Good job!" I became enraged!

How could he be bragging about his role in the slaying of my sister? I pulled my hands slowly away from the bushes and I sat down with my legs crossed in the grass and thought. Of course I didn't hear him actually *say* that he was responsible for Nancy's death, but I was sure of it now and I vowed to make him pay dearly for her death.

Monday morning my mom was making sure I would be at Bible school. After she woke me she saddled me down for the revolting oatmeal, again. God! I hated oatmeal by now, why didn't she ever make eggs basted in butter? Or pancakes swimming in maple syrup? Then at 5 minutes till, I ran down to the church where there were about 10 other kids all waiting for the day to begin. The youth pastor, Bill, got to the church a few minutes late, with his hair messy and his coffee mug in tow. We sang some songs and listened to Bill testify, it was all as I figured it would be, then he let us go precisely at noon.

There was one girl I had never seen before, she didn't say a word to me during the services but when we started to walk back home it seemed we were going the same way. She said,

"Hello!" and I said 'Hi' back.

Then she said, "That was lame. Did your mom make you come, too?"

I smiled, maybe she was new the to neighborhood, so I returned with a voice that made my confession all the more plausible.

"OH, you know it! Yeah, my mom made me come. Do you live around here?"

"Yesem, we moved here a week ago, we waited till it was summertime, so I wouldn't miss any school, how incredibly brainless is that?"

I introduced myself and she said, "That's cool. My name is Laura. Would you like to hang out some time?"

I assured her that I would indeed, that we could hang later today, if she wanted. She said she would and I pointed out which house I lived in so she could come over at 3. She stopped as quickly as she started, then said, "Isn't that the murder house?"

I whispered, "Yes. It is. That was my sister."

She thought about it for a minute, then said, "That's *so* cool! I'm not going to tell me mom where I'm going, but I absolutely love to come over- you said 3, right?"

I was pleasantly surprised by her reaction, and said that the time was right. Then we both went to our separate homes for a few hours.

I walked into the house and Mom immediately stopped ironing and asked, "Well?"

I wasn't sure what she meant by this question and I looked at her for clarification, she went on,

"I mean Bible school-how was it?"

"Okay." then I looked down at my shoes and said, "If it's okay with you, I met this girl named Laura and she's going to come over later."

Mom looked pleased. This was confusing to me as she never had looked like she had any regard for my happiness before.

"Okay," she said, "That's nice that you met someone on your first day." then she continued ironing my dad's handkerchiefs once again.

I went to my bedroom and sprawled myself on the bed for a quick nap. I had an awful dream about Nancy, for a few minutes I thought it was happening for real, in this minute, not just in my dreams, but in real life. First I saw her ghost- but it wasn't like a ghost you would normally see; it was her

bloody and battered ghost. She was fighting off Walter,

whom I was sure about his guilt. I could see his breath,

heavy and nasty, I could actually *see* the breath coming

out of his mouth, lingering in the summer air. I waited to

hear her scream as her mouth was open, but all I heard

was a screeching noise, like a crow in distress. Then

when he finished her off she laid there, and a grackle

walked over to her body and casually picked out her eye

Then he turned and looked right at me with her eye

hanging from his long beak, her eye then turned upwards,

and then right through me.

When I woke I was sweating profusely. I realized it

was a dream, but it was a dream firmly planted in the

present. I stepped over to my window and peeked out of

the small crevice I had left from before. It was stormy

outside, it had started raining while I slept. Suddenly, out

of nowhere, Nancy's ghost returned! Right on the other
side of the window-looking back at me, no, *staring right
through me!* I tried to cry out, but no noise came out. I
shuddered. It took all my strength to reach up and pull the
curtains closed. I walked a few steps backwards, still
looking at the window, fell on the bed and closed my eyes.
I must still be dreaming! I must! I lay there trembling,
afraid to move, afraid I might make a move that would
bring her back into my room. I laid there so long I finally
fell back to sleep and this time I had *no* dreams- none at
all.

At three o'clock my mom knocked on my door and
said, "Your friend is here."

I jumped up and made my way to the dresser. My face
looked like I had been crying. I ran the brush through my
tangled hair and put a smile on my face. I ran to the front
door and there was Laura. She was beautiful;

ethereal would describe her. Her long honey blonde hair went to the middle of her back and she had stunning grey-blue eyes. She wasn't like anyone I had ever met before, and I felt exhilarated being in her presence.

"Hey Laura!" I tried to sound up but she could tell right off that something was wrong.

"What's wrong?" she said with a soft Texas twang, I looked into her eyes and lied,

"Nothing. What could be wrong?"

"Well you look like you've been crying. Tell me." I sat there, not moving.

"Come with me." she said and started walking towards the ravine. I could smell something elusive and faint, she must be wearing perfume, Jasmine, that was the scent, and I found it intoxicating. We climbed down until we got to the bottom of the hill and she started again.

"Okay. We're away from your house so you can talk

now. What's the deal?"

"I was sleeping. I guess that's the way I look when I wake." I said. She wasn't buying this.

"Come on! I know that you had a murder here a couple weeks ago! Tell me, my mom won't let me watch the news." she pleaded. I have to talk to someone.

"Alright. It was my little sister who was killed. She was torn apart, literally. The police were talking about a former inmate from this mental asylum that closed. But, I think if it closed then the inmates are all gone, right?"

"My god!" she said, "But you don't think it was an inmate, do you have an idea about who you think did it?"

I thought for a minute. Was it safe to tell her who *I* thought was the killer? Should I tell her?

"I have my ideas."

"Okay, then share!"

"This is what happened." I started, "I followed the

three of them, Nancy, that's my little sister, Margo, my cousin, and Walter. They went down to tunnel where no one could see them,"

"No one but you, right?" she interrupted.

"Right. I overheard them talking." I paused, "The girls were asking which of them he liked better."

"Ah."

"He said he liked Nancy better, then Margo took off and said she would return in 20 minutes. That's when I left. When I came back an hour later the police where here, she had been killed. Whoever murdered her did it in that time frame. That's why I think it might be Walter."

"So who's Walter? The neighborhood geek?"

"Walter Couly. He lives across the alley from me, and I guess I have standards because I would never have gone to the bottom of the ravine with him."

"So," Laura said slowly, considering every word, "You

didn't think your sister had *standards*. That's pretty harsh. How old was she?"

"Nancy was thirteen. That's my cousin's age as well. Walter is fourteen, same as me, we're in the same grade at school."

"This is starting to come together. Your cousin and this Walter don't tell the police that they were with Nancy-why didn't *you* tell the police what you knew?"

This wasn't good. She was smart.

"I have to wait and see what they have up their sleeves. They must be up to something, they have to be." I said and I turned away, not letting her see what my reaction would be.

"Come on," she said grabbing my elbow, "show me the tunnel!"

I went with her 100 feet to the train tunnel and showed her the underpass. But there were clothes and eating utensils strewn about. This was odd. The police had the place cleared out when they picked up Nancy's body. Everything went as evidence, but now it was back. Surely someone wasn't living here? Laura noticed the same thing. I also noticed for the first time a sewer lid, they must have uncovered it when they picked up Nancy's body.

"The police took what was here before?" she asked, I nodded.

"Well then, we have a mystery! Because it looks like someone else is sleeping here. Weird, though."

"Why?"

"Because why would a person come down here when you know there had been a dead body here?"

I answered, "We're here, aren't we?"

"True enough."

Then I saw the bushes move outside the tunnel. I grabbed Laura by the arm and put my hand over my mouth to keep from screaming.

But it was to late. There was an old man with the stench of the demented reeking from his body. His hair was gray and what little he had stood on end like a clown. He yelled at us, "What in the hell? You screws get outta here, *now!*" he lurched forward and grabbed me by the leg, but I kicked hard and straight into his face. He yelped like a hurt puppy. But I was sure of what he would try to do to us if he caught us. I saw his face, skin weathered like the elastic gone from a balloon, and his teeth, what little he had were stained a deep yellow with seaweed between them-he smelled like the bottom of a trash can.

Laura and I ran up the side of the ravine onto where my street ended, and ran straight up, with the old man with bozo type hair, running behind us. He stopped and limped back. Laura and I looked at each other, so many questions asked in silence. Then, out of nowhere we started laughing. I don't know why, but we suddenly thought it was funny. Maybe it was because he was no where to be seen, perhaps we both thought it was a figment of our imaginations.

Laura said, "We have a mystery and a gully tramp! This is too much."

She put her hand of my shoulder and said,

"Whew! That was more excitement than I've had in ages." We walked up the street and she continued,

"My mom doesn't like me to see the darker side of life, but I think it's the most fun; like going down where your sister died, I am simply fascinated with things like that. Maybe I can help you figure out who did it?" she asked like she was asking me for a bite of candy.

"I know that you already have your suspicions about Walter and your cousin, what's her name again?"

"Margo." the name tasted like poison on my tongue.

83

"Hmm. Margo and Walter, they are our suspects so far...." she said as she rubbed her chin. Then she
said,

"Opps! I forgot. I have to be home in 10 minutes. Bye, y'all!" then she was off. Her hair danced like golden rays, she was something else.

I slowly walked back to my front yard, waving to my mom inside the house, but looking out the window for what I assumed was me. We had a tall tree, a maidenhair, in our front yard and it served it's purpose as a shade maker. I lay underneath the weird leaf shape leaves, thinking about what my sisters last thoughts might have been. I wondered what she had thought when Walter descended on her, tearing and ripping through her skin like it were sheets of linen, instead of a living human being. I hated Walter; hated him with more disdain than I ever thought I could have for another person. And it

84

wasn't just because he had killed my sister-oh, no! There was more to this feeling than that, it was because of his popularity with the other stupid neighborhood kids, the smug look on his face that I longed to slap.

Then there was the time when he put a tack on the teacher's chair, and all the kids laughed when she sat down. Everyone except me, I thought it was reprehensible. And when Mrs. Ashton asked who did it, and no one answered, she said that the whole class was going to pay by keeping us from going out for recess, I raised my hand and told her it was Walter! I did not think it was fair for the whole class to suffer when Walter was the guilty party. But I ultimately paid the price, because none of the kids wanted to be friends with a tattletale, like I had become. I could not understand why he was such a person that people looked up to-didn't they ever see him when he was younger, when he was a ragged brat wandering the alley in bare feet? How could Nancy, my very own sister, be

caught up in him?

I laid there till the sun went down behind the

mountains, and cast it's shadow over me. Then the

street lights came on and I knew I'd better get inside

before Mom had another fit. That night at dinner Jolene

was trying to make conversation, as Mom and Dad were

unusually quiet.

"I heard from a source that the police were desperately

trying to make contact with some old man who's been

seen around the tunnels."

Mom dropped her spoon, and dad gave Jolene a look.

But she continued,

"I heard another person say that he was seen chasing a

couple of girls there only today." she gave me a sideways

glance.

Oh god! She knows it was me! Please don't tell...please

86

don't tell...

"But who these girls were are a mystery to me." she said as she continued to eat her pork chop, thin and dry they were as unappetizing as usual, but it was one of the only times we had meat.

"Umm.." Mom started, "Jolene, I don't think that is proper dinner conversation."

"But I..."

"Drop it!" Dad snarled and again gave her that disapproving cold look of his.

Jolene mumbled as she continued to eat silently. I turned bright red, but I don't think anyone even noticed me, I was invisible. What was proper dinner conversation anyway? What do you talk about when your sister, their daughter has been murdered?

Chapter 8

Later that night, when we had all gone to bed, I heard a quiet tapping on my door.

"Come in." I said.

It was Jolene. She came into my room and silently closed the door behind her.

"I suppose you know you were the one that was seen at the tunnel?" she asked.

"Yeah, I do. I was afraid you were going to tell Mom and Dad at dinner."

"I was." she admitted, "Then they told me to be quiet, so I let it be."

"Why would you tell on me, Jo?" I anxiously said, "What have I ever done to you?" I looked at her with pleading eyes.

"Because I don't want what happened to Nancy to happen to you! Of course I would have told Mom and Dad of your whereabouts if they would have given me half a chance. But, they didn't." she suddenly had the look of a little child. "It's like we don't exist-we're memories for them, from before, when Marcus and Nancy were here."

She had mother's look to her eyes, a twinkle before- a void now. I felt sorry for her, and I went over and sat next to her on my bed. She started to cry. I walked over to the lights and shut them off, then I went to the bed again and took her hand and held on until her cries had subsided.

"Jolene," I asked, "who's been telling you what the police are finding out?"

"A friend of mine. He's a nice guy, really. His name is Mitch. I have never brought him around here because I don't want him getting the third degree from Dad. His brother is a cop and he knows we're related." she heaved with a quiet sigh.

"Mitch, huh?"

"Yup. He told me all about the mental asylum, too."

"He knew about the criminal asylum? Tell me more...I mean about the asylum."

"He told me the most awful stories. Worse than the ones I told you before."

I paused. *What stories? I only remember one...*

"You only told me *one.* The one about how they were running out of funds and the inmates would run through the joint naked."

"Oh, that's right. Well the other ones he told me about were even worse." Jolene said as she was becoming more visible in the moonlight that was streaming through the windows. I could see the outline of her face, tired and weak.

"Well," I asked, "tell me what you've heard."

"He told me the story about how a dozen children were killed by doctors. For a short time they admitted children for special tests they were running. They were wild children, of course-but they were still children. The doctors claimed they didn't mean to poison them, but in giving them a chemical they believed to be good for their mental illness, killed them instead." she whispered, then went on, "He told me stories about the night they were murdered. How their howls and cries went unheeded, how they were throwing up, some of them choking on their own vomit-grisly, barbaric tales. The doctors didn't even realize that those were cries for help, until it was too late."

I put my hand to my mouth as if to stop the screaming in my head.

"Did they get away with that? Weren't there any consequences?" I said as I moved my hand down to my throat.

"It seems that because they were doctors and the children were all considered mentally unstable, that yes, they were able to get away with killing the children with minimal slaps on the wrists. I don't think the doctors even got more than an unsatisfactory paper in their files."

"That's insane!"

Jolene nodded in agreement. "They say the asylum is cursed, you know. Who was the girl you were seen with today?" she asked.

"Oh, her." I said, "She's a girl I met at Bible school today."

"That's nice. At least you made a friend."

"What's that supposed to mean?" I could feel myself getting angry. My hands were starting to sweat, and I tried to wipe it off on my pajamas.

"Nothing. All I meant was that you are always by yourself. I thought you liked it that way."

"I think we'd better change the subject. Tell me what else this 'Mitch' told you." I laid back on the bed wrapping my arms around the pillow.

"Okay. I'll tell you, but you have to promise not to tell anyone about this."

"I promise." I lied, for I knew I would be telling this morsel to Laura tomorrow.

"Mitch told me about a woman who was an inmate at Hell-stratten, her name was Emme. Emme went for a walk one evening around the grounds and she disappeared. The staff went nuts looking for her, but they could not find her. They finally set off the alarm, thinking that she had escaped. They looked for her for two weeks before they finally found what happened to her."

"What did happen to her?"

"They found bits of her body in three different graves. There was another inmate, I forget his name, who was waiting for her to walk past his hiding place on the grounds, behind a large bush, where he attacked her. He

93

chopped her body to bits, hiding it in the graves he had pre-dug behind the same bushes. There was blood all over the back of the bush where he chopped her up, he was naked when he attacked her, and he was able to sneak back into his room and wash the blood off himself." she grimly recalled.

"How did they know it was him?"

"Because of what they found on him."

"Which was?" I leaned closer, totally swept into this story of Hell-stratten.

"Teeth. He kept six of her teeth under his mattress. He would take them out and handle them like they were jewels. One of the attendants found him admiring them, and confiscated the teeth right there. When asked why he had her teeth, he said because she had a beautiful smile. That's the reason-because she had a beautiful smile." she slowly wound up her tale.

"But how did they know he had killed her? Just because he had some *teeth.*"

"Because the lunatic admitted it! He was *deranged!* He made it sound like he was doing her a favor, she never fit in here, he said, she always had an 'air' about her...made him think that she was too good for this place," she said, "so he killed her. Showed them where he buried the body parts."

I was taken aback. "No way! You made that one up!"

"Yes, way! I couldn't make stuff like that up-there's no way I could."

"I find that hard to believe. Did he really mean that? That he killed her because she acted too good for the asylum?" I asked her with my disbelief evident.

"Yeah, he meant it. It's so weird. People actually becoming *attached* to a place like Hell-stratten. You see it all the time, like when a person gets kidnapped and then become attached to their kidnappers. It's like Patty Hearst, first she was kidnapped then she joined them, it's all over the news. Tell me that isn't weird."

"Stockholm syndrome. Yeah, I've heard of it."

"That's right! Hey, you're not as dumb as you look." she jokingly said to me as she punched my arm. We sat in the darkness without saying a word until *it* happened.

A shadow crossed the window, it looked like it was tall, at least taller than I. I grabbed Jolene's arm and made a quiet sound with my finger to my mouth. The shadow looked to be a man, but it had a funny shaped head. Was that a clown's head? The shape was round with floofy puffs of hair jutting out all over. But that's all Jolene and I could make out, the shadow moved about like it was trying to find a way in. Shivers traveled up my spine and I could tell that Jolene was frightened out of her wits. After we watched the shadow move to Jolene's window, we moved to my window to peek outside and see if we could get a grip on what he was doing. He found a small opening in Jolene's window and carefully made it wider. Jolene started to scream bloody murder! We saw the shadow run away across our yard and our dad came bounding into the room.

"What is it? What's wrong?" he yelled. You could see that he was not pleased by having to run upstairs to see what was the problem. Jolene went first,

"Dad! Oh, Dad-there was a shadow moving across my window, and we saw it trying to break in. That's when I screamed." Jolene had run to Dad and put her arms around him. He promptly threw her arms down and said, "Let's go look at your window. I swear Jolene, if this is some kind of joke..."

"I swear, Dad- I swear!" Jolene screamed again.

When we walked into Jolene's room and threw on the

light it was apparent what we said had happened wasn't a lie; for Jolene's curtain was blowing in the breeze and her window was open about 3 inches. Dad's mouth opened wide but he didn't say a thing- for about one minute. Then he started, "Holy shit! Looks like whoever it was, was going to try to break in!" he went over to the window and examined the opening.

"Yeah, you can see it right here. A screwdriver made the initial opening," then he went into the hallway and came back with a flashlight. He opened the window so his head could look out, and then said, "Look here! In the mud outside your window, there are footprints."

Jolene and I looked at each other, and both froze.

"Jesus H. Christ!" he said as he he ran his fingers through his hair, then he went on, "I don't think whoever it was will be back tonight. You two go to bed."

I know that sounds rough, but not if you knew my dad.

When he left us standing there Jolene's mouth made an 'O' shape, but nothing came out. Then it did.

"I can't believe he's going to leave us here. There's someone out there who killed Nancy, and that someone is *still trying to get us now!* But Dad doesn't care, does he? He's leaving us here *alone!"*

"It's okay, Jolene. It's okay. You can sleep in my room, the both of us will look out for one another." I took her by the hand and led her to my room.

"But my window- don't you think we should close it?"

"Yes, maybe we better. Then let's look for a nail, a couple of nails- and close both out windows for good."

"We'll have to find a rubber hammer, so we don't wake up Dad." Jolene started getting color back in her cheeks,and she sounded alive again.

So for the rest of that night, Jolene and I slept huddled close, *after* we nailed both windows shut.

Chapter 9

Jolene woke up just before I did. We were glad to see that the dark of the night gave way to the cool light of morning. Everything looked eerie, even though it was the next day. We went before breakfast to check out the footprints outside Jolene's window. They were there, dried footprints from my window to her's, then further apart as to indicate running away-towards the alley. And that's not all, they were *mens footprints!* Not fully grown men's shoes, however-but you could tell it wasn't a women's shoe.

I stepped into one of the prints with my shoe, just to be sure. Jolene said,

"What are you doing?"

"Checking to make sure it wasn't a woman's shoe. See? The shoe that made these dried prints is much larger than mine, it looks like a kind of boot print." I muttered.

"You can see the heel mark, and the way the shoe is shaped. Whoever it was ran away scared."

"How can you tell?" Jolene asked while she took a closer look.

"You can see the prints are much further apart, as if they were running out of our yard. Too bad there's grass in the rest of the yard, or we would be able to see what direction he ran off."

"How did you get to be so smart?" Jolene asked me with a hint of pride. That made me feel good, a feeling that was foreign to me.

"Reading books. Sherlock Holmes and other stuff." I admitted.

"Oh." she said, "I was so scared last night. Dad was *so not* a help. Thanks for being my rock last night." she sighed, "I guess it's more than I deserve."

"Why do you say that?"

"Because I had been saying that you're being a brat for being scared on previous nights. Because I haven't been a very good sister to you." Jolene's eye's became shiny, as if she were ready to cry. But she didn't cry. Instead, she took a deep breath and squared her shoulders and started walking inside. From over her shoulder she said,

"Do you want oatmeal?"

"Sure," I said, "oatmeal's fine." I was confused.

Did Jolene apologize to me? It sounded as if she did, but I had never seen her tell anyone, let alone me, that she was sorry.

I walked over to the back gate and observed that it was still open from last night. The dirt in the alley was dry, not like the flower beds under the window that had been moistened the night before. But even still, I could see muddy tracks left from shoes that had been wet the night before. And those tracks disappeared into Walter's backyard!

Now I was sure of it, sure that Walter knew about my sister's death, sure that *he was involved,* sure that he *committed* my sister's murder. There was nothing else for me to think. I knew about the lies he told on the day Nancy died, I knew about Margo's lies as well. He had been watching our house every night, I knew everything. The police were so sure it was a crazy person from the asylum, but only *I* knew the whole truth. And I was damn sure I was going to make Walter pay.

Chapter 10

After breakfast I put on my denim jacket and went to the back gate. Walter was in his yard, smoking with his motley crew when I approached.

"I need to talk to you." I said looking directly into Walter's eyes.

"Yeah? What about?" he said with his swagger intact. He flicked his cigarette on the ground, then stomped it to put it out.

"Not here. Not in front of your...friends." I said.

"Do you want to come into my room?" Walter laughed, his friends laughed too. "I'm sure I can get you in through the window."

"Ow! Walter she's not the one you wanted, right?" his fat friend Peter boy said. I squinted, what exactly does this mean?

"Peter boy," I started, "Isn't this the day you're

supposed to shave your palms?" he looked vacant-just like his friends, he knew nothing. "No, I've had enough Cro-magnon stereotypes tell me what to do today. " I was disgusted. *'Damn Neanderthals!'* "Go on now, I think the bus for the fat camp is here-you don't want to miss it."

"Then where do you want to go?" Walter walked up to me, about a foot taller than I. I was not impressed.

"Down to the end of the alley. Just where the ravine starts."

"I don't want to go there. I don't like it there." Was there a flicker of fright?

"Then tell your friends to go away, I don't want ears around."

Walter shooed his friends away, and then we were left there alone in his backyard.

"Walter," I began, "why have you been watching our house since the day of the murder?"

"I don't know what you're talking about. I haven't been watching your house. Why would I?"

"I can tell by the footprints, I can tell by the man's shadow I saw in my window the last two nights- how much more to I have to say? Do I really have to go on?"

"You're crazy! I have done nothing you say. I'm not creeping up to your window at night-you must be imagining things- *again*!"

"What do you mean, *again*?" I spit these words.

"I mean you've been spying on *me*, ever since your sister was murdered. Why don't you leave me alone?" he was shaking. He was afraid, and I knew what he was afraid of.

"I know that you know something about Nancy's murder!" I squarely accused him.

"Look," he started to back away. "I mean it, I had

106

nothing to do with your sister dying like she did. I didn't do it-why don't you leave me alone you crazy bitch?" he ran towards his duplex, falling over his feet as he went.

"I know it was you, and I'll prove it!" I shouted after him. I meant it, too.

What I needed now was Margo. She was the key to unraveling this mystery.

A few days later Margo was dropped off at our house, I guess the grownups had decided that enough time had passed for it to be alright for her visits again. I don't know, how much time does a broken family need to mend itself? Even if it was broken to begin with. Two weeks had passed since the murder and we were no closer to solving the crime than before. At least the police were no closer.

Jolene had kept me informed with her boyfriend's brother had been saying as to what the police were keeping their eyes on

-and it was so backwards that I would laugh when she told me. Jolene would look at me strangely when I laughed, as if this were no laughing matter. Which it wasn't. Maybe she looked at me because this was our sisters murder and I should keep inappropriate laughter to myself.

Margo came into the house and dropped off her stuff in my bedroom, then she went out. I followed her.

"Where are you going, Margo?" I asked.

"Oh, just to wander around the neighborhood, walking."

"I'm kind of glad you're back. I wanted to talk to you."

"What in the world do you want to talk to me about?" she asked.

"About Nancy's death. The circumstances." I looked at her and saw a thin thread of sweat start to form above her eyebrow.

"Nancy's dead now. I don't want to talk about her anymore." she said trying to keep from tripping over her

108

tongue.

I grabbed her by the arm firmly, and took her into the backyard. She came easily at first, but then she started to push me away.

"Get off me!" she said as she pushed my arms off.

"We can talk here." I said, looking around to make sure we were alone.

"Wow, you're so smart. You got me now!" she said sarcastically.

"I wanted to ask you about where you were when Nancy was killed. Don't you think I'm entitled to know? Do you think I'm stupid?" I regretted saying this last.

"Yeah, I do think you're stupid, if you think I'm ever going to tell you a thing! The police have asked their questions, that's all I'm required by law to answer. You can take your questions and shove them right up your...."

Suddenly she stopped talking but her mouth kept on

moving, but there was nothing coming out. Her eyes were fixed on an object behind me: I turned. She was looking towards Walter's backyard, but I could not detect anyone there.

"What do you see? What is it?" I asked.

"Nothing. I see nothing." she said as she hurried out the back gate. "and don't you go around making up stories about me, either!"

Stories? About her? I did not understand. I did notice that she was running towards the ravine, and since the police hadn't arrested her or Walter for the murder, I didn't feel it was safe to come out with my conclusions.

"Margo, wait!" I yelled. I started running after her, but she was already down the vertiginous hill. I saw her running towards the tunnel with her brown hair flying in the wind. There was a small dirt cloud she kicked up as she ran. I tried to yell at her once more.

"Margo, *please* come back!" I was running so hard my lungs ached. I could not let her get away, I had to talk to her today.

She slipped under the railway bridge, I saw her go in. But when I reached it, she was nowhere to be found. I ran around the bridge, then I ran to the top, to the railways. I heard the bells of the rail crossing gate come down. In the distance I saw the train coming- whistling for us to get away; it was 10:00 o'clock; but I could not find Margo.

I started screaming, "Margo! Can't you hear it? The trains coming! We have to get out of here- it's not safe to play here when the trains coming!"

The whistle coming closer, it was at the end of the block and ravine- about 100 yards away. The whistle was getting louder and longer. I was frantic! Surely the train engineer could see me waving my arms, trying to get him

111

to stop in time.

Then the derailment began. At first there was a squealing sound as the engineer hit the brakes, but then it hit the rickety part of the train tracks and the hurling train suddenly became the flying chemicals that would burst into flames at the slightest flame. The train was still coming at me, piling up all the while and bringing the whole burning mess right to me. The train started to be thrown off the tracks, car by car it was piling up in front of me. I heard the sound of metal on metal and saw sparks fly off the trains wheel base. The sparks were all it took to set the cars on fire, and it became a huge orange and red fireball. The sounds the train made were agitated, wild slams, I thought it would never stop. Metal on metal crashing down upon me. It was an explosion to end all explosions! *POW! WHOOSH!*

Now I realized that it was a mistake to try to make the

train stop. It was a maddening mistake! I realized that I might be the cause of a train wreck, and that Margo might be caught in that same wreck. Closer the train came as I flew off the top of the rail bridge, running the whole time. I could hear, because I dared not to look at the train, the awful sounds the freight cars jackknifing on the bridge, swallowing the tunnel whole below the bridge. I could hear and feel the fire that sprung up immediately as the accident progressed. The fire made a huge 'whooosh', and I could feel the heat on the back of my neck. I later found out that it took less than 3 minutes for the entire train to stop- but on that day it seemed to take forever.

I lifted my head, slowly at first. Then I looked at the train and the mess it had caused. There were freight cars loaded with chemical containers strewn everywhere, and the compartment with the engineer was demolished. I could see far to the back of the train, despite the smoke

113

and fire, and it looked like a child's railroad set up awry-with cars knocked off the rails all the way across the street. A fog was rising from the accident scene, and I saw a few fires starting up in the engine. I had the sudden feeling that I was not alone-I felt Marcus's ghost at my side.

'You jumped just in time! I'm glad.' I heard his small voice. I replied, *'Marcus! Where have you been?'*

'I've always been here, always.' I was stunned. I held out my hand to grasp his-and I felt a warm sense holding my hand. It was with a aching hunger that I squeezed back.

Good as that felt, I had to find Margo. I went to the tunnel under the bridge, which was difficult to get to because I had to get past the freight cars, and I started to look frantically.

"Margo, are you here?" I tried to push past wreckage,

114

but it was hot to touch. I peered around the pile in front of me and I saw hair-not just human hair, Margo's hair! It was a ghastly find, for it wasn't attached to a body. Her lifeless form had been thrown and covered with scratches over into the far section of the tunnel. Margo's head had been stripped from her body, leaving her deformed and disfigured. I heard the police and fire sirens, they were moments away. I realized that Marcus was gone as well.

Should I stay here with Margo, even though she was dead? I admit that I was scared that the police would question me about our relationship, and what the hell we were doing in the ravine merely a couple weeks after my sister died. I ran in the opposite direction, positive that no one had seen me go down to the tunnels.

No one had, except for one person. Laura.

Chapter 11

I was surprised to see Laura, as I rose from the fog.

"Laura." I said, my breath catching in my throat.

"Whoeee! You caused that accident, didn't you? I saw ya down on the tracks just before it crashed. Why were you waving your arms like that, all crazy like?"

Laura, it seems, was fascinated by the crash.

"Don't worry, y'all. I won't tell that I saw you, but why did you do that, wave your arms?"

"Oh, Laura, I have to tell someone, or I'll burst." I said as I was walking up towards the end of her street which also dead- ended into the ravine. I pulled my arm up and wiped the sweat off my brow, making grease smear across my face.

"Come on, let's get you washed up before they start looking for you." and I followed her like a lost puppy.

We went into her bathroom, strewn with pictures of

cowgirls riding horses, and I filled my hands up with cool water, then splashed my face. It felt so good, so cool, and so far away from the accident, and I was grateful. I caught a glimpse of myself in the bathroom mirror, I looked ghastly. My hair was not it's usual lank brown pageboy mop, instead it was transformed into a frizzy mane of a girl I did not recognize. The fire had done it's number on me, I needed to wash myself off. I decided to tell her everything.

"It started this morning, a while ago, really." It spilled from there. "Margo came over to my house again, apparently her folks thought it was safe again." I gulped the air as I continued. Laura gave me a paper cup filled with the cool water to drink.

"I asked her what her role was in Nancy's murder."

Laura slapped me on the back and made a 'whoeee' noise again.

"You came right out and asked her? Boy, you *are* brave."

I looked around for Laura's mother, I didn't see her.

"Are we alright? I mean, I don't see your mother." I asked.

"Don't worry about her old ass! She's working at the hospital til late tonight. Go on with your story."

I had the sudden urge to ask where her father was, but I had the feeling that it was just Laura and her mother. So I went on.

"After I asked Margo about her role in the murder she looked over my shoulder with the weirdest look in her eyes."

"Like she was guilty of something?" Laura asked.

"Yes...no. Like she had seen something that really scared her. Terrified her..."

"And?"

"Then she ran off, towards the ravine. I ran after her but she was too fast and she disappeared under the rail bridge. I ran towards the bridge, too, but when I got there it was empty! No one was there."

"Then what happened?"

"Then I couldn't find her anywhere. I called her name over and over. But I could not find her. Then I heard the whistle of the train, it was coming towards us. I remembered what my father told us, 'Don't play in the ravine when the trains coming through, it's dangerous.'" I stopped. I did not think I could go on, but I did.

"The train whistle. That's all I could hear, so I started to wave my arms like I was mental, trying to make it stop. Then I realized that it was a mistake, to make it stop in that short of time would cause an accident, that the train would hit the unstable track that ran over the bridge, that the cars would pile up on top of each other. I jumped off the bridge just in time for it to miss me and I heard the awful noise behind me. I had to put my hands over my ears because it was so loud. When it stopped I looked once again for Margo, fearing that she might have been trampled in the wreck." I looked at Laura, her face was almost euphoric.

"Don't stop now, finish!"

"I found Margo." I stuttered.

"Where was she hiding?" she asked. I realized that I was in shock, but I went on.

"She wasn't hiding, I saw her *head*, I saw her *body*. *They were torn apart!* Under the bridge, it's still there, they will find it in a few minutes, if they haven't already. I ran, until I ran into you." I started to heave, I was going to be sick.

"Here-lift the toilet lid." Laura said. But I wasn't sick, I wasn't feeling anything.

"Can I say that I was here with you the whole time?" I asked Laura, unsure of how complicit she wanted to be with the police and their questions.

"What the hell? I'll cover for you. Heck, I even saw you down there waving your arms- I don't have any reason to doubt your story." She patted me on the back and then ran her fingers through her long honey-blonde hair.

"Thanks. You're a good friend." I said.

"Sure. We'll have to think of what we were doing. Like playing chess." Laura said.

"I don't know how to play chess." I said.

"That's why I'm teaching you, silly! Now get the chess board out and set up the pieces." she said as she reached into the game closet. I ran the cool water through my hair and began to towel it off.

"Okay, now the board is set up, that's our alibi." Laura said with a sneaky smile, "Now we are going to have to

121

stroll up to the accident, like we're curious about the noise the train made, *AND* we're going to have to *act* like we're surprised! Remember, you don't know where Margo is, you came here right after breakfast. You got that, right?"

"I think so. I hope I can act now, I'm so nervous." I said as I rubbed my elbows.

"Just come with me. We'll go out now and *remember this-we're surprised as anyone as to Margo's whereabouts.*" she said as she grabbed my arms, "Come on."

We walked across her yard and up to the edge of the hill. It was a bloody mess! The police had arrived first, then the fire department. They had their hoses out, but had determined that the fires in the train engine would be best put out with the foam they carried. The policemen were waiting for the fire to be extinguished, but you could see in the engine, where the dead engineer lay crushed, the ambulance drivers didn't make haste—they *knew* he was dead, as his lifeless corpse lay hunched over the window.

"Oh thank god!" it was my mom's voice. "Have you seen Margo this morning? I can't find her, and I've looked everywhere." her voice was shaky.

"No, mom. I've been with Laura all morning, right?"

"Yes, as a matter of fact I'm teaching your daughter to play chess." Laura smiled like a madwoman.

"If you do see Margo, tell her to come home right away." and off she went asking all the neighborhood children the same question.

"You did great! Did you see? She didn't even question us."

I did not take her reply as a vote of confidence, for I knew that any second one of the policemen would be going through the train wreck and he would find Margo.

"I need to get out of here." I whispered loudly at Laura.

"Hold your horses, I want to look a little bit more." She was looking at the train wreck with unnerving eyes. I looked away. We must have been an odd sight that day, both of us standing together but looking in different directions, neither of us daring to see what the other saw.

"Oh!" Laura said, "The fireman are done, they've finished putting the foam down. And here comes the police."

"Can't we leave?" I pleaded.

"You're such a baby!" she said, "We can leave in few more minutes. Look!" she said pointing out my mom standing of the edge of the ravine, the closest the police would allow. Mom was looking directly at the bridge, or more directly at the tunnel underneath, as if she already knew what the police would find. I could see her, almost like standing in a time machine where I could keep her the

124

way she was, but knowing that it was real- and that it was a matter of minutes before I saw her crushed, again.

She was biting her nails with vigor, and I knew that her nails were already bitten off down to the beds, and they were now or already bloody. Mom had been biting them for the past couple weeks, since Nancy's death. What was she going to do now? Keep on biting them down past the beds, down to the finger bone?

"One cop is going up to the engineer, I think he's already found him. But look here!" Laura said pointing to the tunnel, "That cop is going under the train wreckage, to the tunnel."

"Oh god!" I wailed.

I hadn't even noticed that my mom was looking at us, particularly Laura, who was pointing to where the action was proceeding.

"Look, look!" Laura said as she grabbed me by the

125

shoulders and pointed me at the tunnel. "That cop found her, he found her!"

The policeman got on his radio and said what I could only imagine. For the next few minutes the area swarmed with policemen coming into the sight, yellow tape going up, cops yelling for us to leave the area-but we all stayed.

Mom started to shriek, "Why are you putting yellow tape up-where's my niece? Have you found her? Have you?"

The policeman who was standing up near the end of our street said unknown words into his microphone then proceeded in holding Mom back. For she was trying to run down the ravine to find out what happened.

Suddenly cops came out of nowhere. There were 7 cops running up the side of the ravine in half a minute to hold my mom back.

Mom was trying to break through, crying as she went,

trying every trick she could think of to find out what was
happening.

"You don't understand," Mom cried, "My daughter
died here two weeks ago! I am...I was her mother."

One of the policemen must have recognized her and he
came to her rescue.

"Easy boys! She's right. She was the mother of the girl
that died here a few weeks ago." He took off his cap,
"How are you doing, ma'am?"

Mom wiped her tears and said, "I'm trying to find my
niece! She's missing and that cop down there is putting up
yellow tape, just like you did with my daughter."

"Why don't you stay up here, with my fellow officers
while I try to find out why he's putting up the tape, okay?"

"I'll stay, but not for long!"

The policeman put his cap back on and proceeded to
walk towards the tunnel. I knew what the cop found

already, *I knew.* The cop walked down to the creek, to the tunnel and I saw him take his hat off and brushed it hard against his legs. He looked up towards my mother, then I saw his head fall. He took a few seconds before he started to walk up to where my mother stood, waiting.

"Let's move a little closer, Laura. I want to hear what he says." I whispered inaudibly.

"Good idea. We can hear him tell her that it's a girl's body they found." Laura said pumping her fists. I suddenly felt like a ghoul. I knew what he was going to say, and I knew that my mom was going to crumble. I didn't want to stay one more minute, I couldn't stand myself. I grabbed Laura by the arm and I twisted her back towards her house.

"What are you doing? Don't you want to stay and see what's going on?" Laura asked.

I couldn't stay and I wanted her to say she knew the

reason. But she didn't and I felt such a fool.

"I can't believe that you would *want* to stay and see my mother crumble! Have you no decency?" I roared.

"Don't talk to me about decency-you're the one who caused this whole mess! I only wanted to see where she looked after they told her, you know? She must have suspicions about someone in the neighborhood? Don't you want to see if Walter is there?" Laura asked with a sense that made me think there was more than she had noticed. I hadn't thought of looking for Walter, or to see if Mom had thought of him as a suspect.

"Maybe you're right." I said, "I wasn't thinking. Maybe if we hurry back we can see the officer tell my Mom."

"Now you're talking!" she said and we started running back just in time to hear the officer ask Mom if her niece had long brown hair, and was about 5 feet tall. Mom said yes to both questions and I heard her ask why he asked.

I heard him tell her that there was indeed a young girl fitting that description involved in an accident. I couldn't hear what Mom asked him next, I did see her fall completely apart- she asked through the tears if she was still alive. The cop shook his head and then caught Mom in his arms. She had passed out. He motioned for the ambulance personnel to come pick her up and I scoured the people who were there watching the madness. Most of the neighborhood was there, Carla and Cyndi stood like twin statues, but I could not find Walter among them.

"I don't see Walter. Do you see him?" I asked.

"No. I don't. I don't see him, do you know what that means?"

"What does that mean?" I asked, my curiosity peaked.

"If the perpetrator isn't among the people present, it must be because he's hiding something big. *Like he's hiding the truth?* It means he was probably in a place he shouldn't have been-like the tunnel! He's probably off wiping his hands, getting rid of evidence!" Laura turned around and kept hitting her fist into her hand.

"You're right! Laura, I don't think you really meant it, but I think that you're right!"

"What do y'all mean by that? Of course I meant it."

"I'm sorry. It's just that I..."

"Forget it, I know y'all were just in shock-it happens when you go through an trauma, hell, catastrophe! My mother told me all about that." she said proudly. I took this as an opening to find out about her and her mom.

"You said your mom's a nurse. Where does she work?" I asked.

"Denver General, it's an enormous place."

"What department does she work?"

"She works with the mental patients. Their pretty full

down there, ever since her other place was shut down."

"What *other* place?" I asked as a creepy shiver went down my spine. I had a feeling I already knew the answer.

"A huge place, a mental asylum over in Lakewood, about a mile and a half from here. They closed it down because they said it was too expensive to run. I guess there were a lot of things wrong with the place, pipes leaking, heater kept breaking down-so one day they just shut it down."

"What was the *name* of the asylum?"

"Oh, you wouldn't believe me anyway." she said. I was getting angry now.

"WHAT WAS THE NAME OF THE ASYLUM?" I spit through my teeth.

"Heilstratten. Or more widely known as Hell-stratten."

Hearing the name took my breath away. *Hell-stratten.* I had to ask.

"Do you know what they did with the patients? I mean I've heard of the place, but I haven't heard good things about the place. I've heard it was cursed. I heard they just opened the gates and let the inmates onto the streets." I said, trying not to show how upset I was.

"It wasn't quite like that, you know, where they opened up the gates and let people out. Some of the patients, the ones that were there for criminal reasons, were transferred to other asylums. Some escaped as the day drew near, they didn't think anyone would care about them if they lived quietly on their own. But there were quite a few that were turned out onto the streets, I'm sad to say." for a second, she did *look* sad. "And I would call it haunted, not cursed."

"So you're saying that there are some crazy's living on the street, but most of the patients were transferred to other places?"

133

"That's what I'm saying. Oh, there was the legend of the pick ax murderer. You know, the one that got away."

"The pick ax murderer?" I slowly said.

"Yes. I heard that he had a favorite tool. The pick ax, and he loved to use it on people-not just any person, mind you-but if you said something bizzare, something he didn't like, then he would jump out of the bushes and slaughter you!" Laura said enjoying the effect her story was having on me. But I had to ask her to continue.

"So he was in the asylum, right?"

"Not at first. They put him in prison, the regular kind, and he continued to find tools that he could use in the same way as a pick ax. Like say he was working in the prison laundry-if a guy pissed him off he would use the tin lids, the sharp edge of the tin lids, to slice a man's head off!"

"NO!"

"Yeah, it's true. But that wasn't the end. They finally took him away from the general population, like his lawyers had been trying to do all along, when he told the guards what he had done. He simply told them that he was outraged at the man for wearing gray that day. That's it, that's the reason-he was wearing gray!"

"Don't all the prisoners wear gray?" I asked.

"Yep."

"And you say he got away?" I was astonished.

"Yes, he did. But that's not what the personnel will tell you. They'll tell you that he mysteriously 'died' one stormy night when the power went out. Sure, that one'll fly."

"So you don't think he died?"

"No, and neither does anyone else. Where's his body? When was his funeral?"

"Maybe they sent his body out of state; they don't

conduct funerals for the patients at the asylum-right?" the very thought of this chilled me to my bones.

"There's a cemetery out back. And yes, they did conduct funerals when a patient died and no one collected their bodies."

"Your mother told you all of this?" I couldn't believe that a mother would 'share' this type of information with her daughter, it was unbelievable.

"She told me some."

"How did you find out the rest? Like it was haunted."

"Oh, I have my ways." she said mysteriously. She jumped up and took me by the hand and led me to her kitchen. "Let's find out what she left for me today, what do you say?"

"Okay." I said coming back to Earth, it suddenly hit me that my house was in a panic.

I guessed Jolene was probably looking for me, as my

mom had been taken to the hospital when the ambulance driver had taken her away.

"Laura," I said not looking her in the eyes, I couldn't say anything-but my eye's always gave me away.

"I better get back to my house. My sister must be looking for me. See ya!"

"Okay, but don't forget."

"Forget?"

"Yeah, that we were playing chess the whole time-remember?"

"I won't forget." I said as I flew out her back door and back to people standing around, when I finally saw Jolene. She looked relieved to see me and she was waving her arms in motion for me to come to her. I made my way over to her and she said, "They took Mom in an ambulance, I didn't even get a chance to talk to her. I was going crazy looking for you!"she paused, "Hey, how did

137

your hair get wet?"

I fixed my face so she wouldn't be able to tell I was hiding a secret. I looked down and replied, "Sorry, I didn't know. I was at my friends house, my new friend Laura." I still refused to look into her eyes, but she didn't notice my subterfuge.

"Come on! We've got to find Margo, I haven't seen her since just after she got here." she slowed down and tried to look me in the eye for the first time.

"Have *you* seen Margo?"

I jumped back and said with all the condemnation I could muster, my eyes widening,

"NO! I have not. Why would you even ask me if I've seen her?" I shouted.

"She's dead, you know. Dead!' I thought. "You know that Margo and Nancy were best friends, *not* Margo and me! She doesn't want to have anything to do with me!"

"Okay- sorry! I just thought, maybe....let's look for her, truce?"

I shook my head. "Perhaps she's back at the house, have you looked there?" I asked feeling badly that I was lying to my only sister now. But it could not be helped.

"I checked at the house. I even asked the people who were on the front street of my house, all the way up and down. I've asked every person I've met. No one has seen her." she said.

I decided to ask her, "Did you ask Walter?"

"Walter? Who's Walter?"

"You know, he's my age and he lives in the duplex behind our house." I tried to make it as vague as possible, so she wouldn't suspect that I had already done so.

"OH, him. No, I haven't seen *him.*" she said as she tapped her fingers on her chin. "but since I found you, let's continue to look for Margo. You go around that way, the long way, and I'll go ahead and ask towards the front. We'll meet in half an hour to exchange information."

She blended into the crowd, asking people as she went, I went straight for Walter's house-there was a question I wanted to ask him, a question that desperately needed an answer.

I marched to his back door and knocked loudly. *Bam,Bam, Bam!!* I saw the curtain move slightly but he didn't answer. I yelled, "Come on out, Walter! I know you're in there, I saw you!"

Finally the swung open and there stood Walter. He was holding an ice cube in a washcloth over his left eye, it was black. Some one had hit him.

"What do ya want? I'm busy." he said.

"A black eye, huh? Where did you get that?" I observed, "Looks fresh."

"None of your beeswax, bitch. I'm going." he started to

close it, but I had stuck my foot in the door.

"What are you doing?" he asked me with his voice trembling. I hadn't noticed before but his other eye was red and watering. He had been crying.

"I wanted to ask you where you have been for say, the last hour? Didn't you hear the train wreck? The whole neighborhood's down there, everyone but you!" I looked him square in the eye.

"I've been nursing my eye, if you must know. I heard the train wreck, but I've been busy taking care of my *ocular socket*, okay?" he was being facetious. Good God, I hated him. He was talking like that because I had won the science award for my work with the human eye, and his sarcasm was *not* appreciated.

"Who gave you the black eye? Margo?" I tried once more.

"Margo? She hasn't been around for weeks."

141

"She was here this morning, *you saw her.* Or at least she saw you! I saw her looking into your yard after breakfast and then she froze, like a statue! She was looking right into *your* yard! What other shenanigans are you pulling?" I argued.

"I don't knows *what she saw, I only know it couldn't have been me!"*

"I can smell it on you! Tell me the truth."

"Because this morning I snapped at my mother. Mother, *huh*! I was mad that she passed out with her bottle of whiskey and cigarettes lit in her hand again. She started a small fire and was lucky I was there. It could have taken the whole duplex down, what with her slobbery alcohol breath. When I was arguing with her, she punched me in the eye! Are you happy now?" he said as he kicked my foot out of the door and slammed it shut.

'Nice excuse!' I thought. Bet he's used that one before.

Everyone knew that his mom was a drunk, and it for sure wasn't the first time she had struck him- *IF she was the one who struck him!*

I looked at the cheap watch I had received from my parents to show that they appreciated me-*not* loved me- they could never do that. I knew the difference. I know that they had purchased that watch for Nancy, as I had overheard them talking about her birthday. Of course, her birthday came and went since she was murdered. I guess my parents didn't want to *waste* a gift.

It was now a half hour and I decided to find Jolene and go on pretending as if I didn't know what happened to Margo.

I took a deep breath and I walked back to the crowd of people being held back by the police. I didn't have to look hard, she was easy to find. I walked up to Jolene and shrugged my shoulders. Immediately she told me, "You

143

didn't find her? Where could she be?"

Carla and Cyndi were standing still, and they heard Jolene. Carla hiccupped, "It's M-argo that's missing, isn't it?"

Jolene looked at Carla and nodded her head. "She's missing. Do you know where she is?"

"Not for sure," Carla said slowly as if to frighten Jolene, "but you know they found another body among the train wreckage, you know that, r-right?"

Jolene appeared as if what Carla said didn't make sense, then it sunk in and she freaked out. Jolene jumped over to Carla and grabbed her shoulders.

"How do you know? Did they tell you that? *How do you know??*" Jolene shouted.

Carla looked surprised by Jolene's attack and returned, "Calm down! I s-saw your mother pass out when they told her something I couldn't hear; but between her being taken to the hospital and the police putting up the yellow tape under the bridge, I assumed."

"You assumed? How can you assume a thing like that?" Jolene sounded like she was going out of her mind. I wanted so much to tell her that Carla was right, that the police *did* find a body, but I kept my promise to Laura and I said nothing.

"Go ask them," Jolene told me, indicating that I should go ask the policeman. "Go, *GO!*"

"I'll go." I said as I approached one of the officers.

"Stay back!" the policeman said, looking very official.

"I don't want to go into the ravine," I said, "I do have some questions I need to ask you."

"Uh huh." he said as he looked around for kids trying to get down the ravine and snoop. NOT on his watch!

"The tape," I said, "yellow tape. My sister was the one they found a couple weeks ago, murdered under the bridge. They used yellow tape for her."

"Oh?" he said, one eyebrow going up.

"Does that yellow tape indicate that you've found *another* body?"

"I'm afraid I can't tell you that. Not until we notify next of kin."

"*I'm her next of kin*, if you did find a body! My cousin is staying with us and she is *missing*! So please tell me, did you find her?" I pleaded, almost to the point of tears.

"Do you have someone who is *older*? Where's your mother?"

"She was taken to the hospital. One of your officers told her something that made her pass out! Now, I'm not a detective or anything, but I think they must have told her that what they found was my cousin!"

I could tell they were not going to tell me a thing, so I called Jolene over. She ran over and told the officer, "I'm her older sister, and yes, my mom is at the hospital."

The officer looked at the both of us, pitying the sight of two sisters who were too young to know the truth. I was about to burst! The officer looked at Jolene for a second and said, "Your name is Jolene, right?"

"Yes, it is."

"I'm Mitch's brother." then he looked around to see if other officers were in earshot, they weren't.

"Just tell us!" I shouted, "did you find a body? Is it of a girl, about 13 years old with brown hair?"

"I guess I can tell you that much," he said quietly, shutting his radio off. "Yes, apparently they found a girl down there, and she wasn't killed by the train wreck. That's all I know," he said again, this time with authority, "Now get lost! You didn't hear it from me!" he said as he shooed us off.

147

"Oh my god! Do you know what this means?" Jolene said as she broke into tears. "This is a disaster!"

"Don't worry, Jolene! Perhaps it wasn't her." I lied.

"But you heard it yourself," she blubbered, "they found a body, it was a girl about the same age. What are we going to tell Aunt Paula?"

"Now you shutup!" I said, I looked at Jolene in her sad eyes, "Even if it is her, you and I don't know it yet! That's Dads job to tell Aunt Paula, *not ours*! Do you hear me? NOT OURS! We're too young to get involved."

"But we are involved! She's involved, I can't stand it!" Jolene kept right on crying. I grabbed her by the head and patted her back.

"What I meant was this- Mom is going to have to call Dad at work and when he sees her in the hospital, she'll tell him then. And Aunt Paula is *his* sister, so you and I don't have to tell her a thing." I soothed her with my explanation.

"But Mom and Dad will want to know why we weren't with her. Where did she go after she got here? Do *you* know?"

I did know, I feigned ignorance. "I have no idea where she went after breakfast. I told you that Margo and I aren't friends. I went to my friends house. She and I were playing chess." I lied once more.

"I was in my room. Do you think Mom and Dad are going to buy that we didn't have any idea of where she went?" her voice crackled.

"Listen," I said , "it's not our job to keep her company, to babysit her. It *not* our job."

"I guess you're right."

"Of course I'm right. Let's keep our heads about us, let's go back to the house and pretend like we know *nothing!*" I urged.

"How can we pretend we know nothing?" she said, "it's impossible."

"You're going to have to get hold of yourself, and remember..."

"Remember what?" she asked.

"Remember to act calm. Can you do that?" I asked her.

"I don't know, I don't know....I can try."

"We are going back to the house. *We know nothing*! Got it? NOTHING!! Let the police contact us about Mom being in the hospital, although they probably won't. They have to contact an adult, which is Dad, and they should get the phone number from Mom-if she can tell them, which I'm sure she will." I told her in a soft, lilting voice as to keep her composed. It was working, she slowly started to breath in a controlled manner.

I put my arm around Jolene and started walking back to the house, from the back alley. I didn't want to walk into

Carla and Cyndi again. They ask way too many

questions. We were at the back gate when there was a

chink of light reflected in my eyes. It was Walter's

window, he had closed it quickly, but I knew it was him. I

knew.

Chapter 12

Jolene and I waited inside, trying to keep busy cleaning the house. That was something we never did unless under duress from our mother. But we had to be doing chores to keep our minds off the fact that out world was once again to crumble around us. We knew when our dad came home, probably accompanied by Mother that the questions would start. We had the t.v. on for background noise, to keep our minds engaged. *Gilligan's Island* was the show that was on, and the upbeat music was a strange dichotomy to reality. It seemed unreal.

I had most of the items pulled out of the hallway cabinet, cleaning the shelves when I heard Dad's car pull into the driveway. Jolene suddenly dropped her dusting cloth and discontinued cleaning the tops of the kitchen cabinets and looked at me with sheer fright. I shook my head at her, put my finger to my mouth and gave her a strong look. She continued to dust with her nerves strung tight and mounting. A moment later the door opened and Mom and Dad walked into the room. I decided to break the silence.

"MOM! Where were you? Jolene and I have been s*oooo* worried."

"Jolene," Dad said, "Please take your mother to her room, she needs to lie down."

"Of course, dad." Jolene said as she jumped down off the counter and gently took Mom by the shoulders. Jolene gave a grave look as she left the room.

"Dad," I started, "what's going on? Where was mom? I tried to keep my wits about me, tried to keep..."

"I think you already know, don't you?" his voice was rough and tattered, as if he had already been crying, but he wasn't going to cry in front of me.

"NO!" I lied again, but this time it was easier. "How

153

could *I know?* I've been here with Jolene all afternoon, wondering what's going on."

"So you know nothing about the train wreck today?" he asked trying to look me in the eye, but I remembered to look at his forehead instead. I read that it was a way to avoid the glare, or intensity trying to be foisted upon me.

"Yes, I know the train wrecked today, everyone knows that! But Jolene and I were looking for Mom among the crowds of people, but we couldn't find her. We imagined the worst."

"The worst *has happened*! Didn't you think to look for your cousin Margo when you were looking in the crowds of people?" His voice was cracking again, but I sensed he was being cynical at the same time.

"I don't understand what you're saying...what happened to Margo?" *Look at his forehead, look at his forehead...*

"Margo is dead! She was killed today, probably by the

154

same monster who killed my baby, Nancy..." he started crying and fell against the kitchen table. I didn't even try to pick him up, I didn't want to touch him. He made it over the kitchen sink and got a drink of whiskey. He was looking out the window, into the street which was starting to buzz with twilight.

"DEAD?" I said with amazement. I was an actor playing a part now...anyone but myself. "How can that be?"

"The police told me that they found her, and your mother told me it was her. I have already talked with my sister, Paula. She fainted dead away." he said in a voice that I had never heard him use. It was completely void of life.

"She fainted, *dead away?*" I asked. I did not know what he meant by that.

"She fainted and hit her head on the edge of the table

when she fell. She's in the hospital now, critical condition...news of her daughters death and now this!"

I wasn't sure what I should say, but I continued. "Oh Dad...I'm sorry. Aunt Paula *and* Margo?"

His face turned from orange to red, snarling his teeth at me.

"Don't go telling me that you're sorry-alright?" his voice came back to life again. Anger mixed with hatred- he was yelling at me. He was acting like *I killed them.* "I'll show you sorry!"

His belt cleared his loops and Dad started hitting me, as if with every snap of the leather he was bringing back to life his sister and niece. I covered my face with my hands, but I refused to cry for him, that's what he wanted. I had too much pride to give him that. My arms were covered with welts and cuts where he had hit me, but he also got me in the face a couple of times. When his arms grew tired he pulled me by the hair and threw me towards my room. My eyes were teary, but I walked into my room with the cavalier attitude I knew I could give. I could hear him whimper, but I knew it wasn't because he was sorry about what he did to me; it was for Paula, Nancy and Margo.

Chapter 13

I was laying in bed later that night, Jolene managed to get to her room without running into Dad. I didn't blame her for hiding, I would have done the same thing if the situation was reversed. I could hear the mumblings of Mom and Dad coming from their room, the vents were famous for listening to people from any other room *if* that's what you wanted. I did not.

Suddenly there was a tap at my window. I froze. I was afraid it was Walter, or the shadow of that man that Jolene and I saw. Then I heard a voice whisper, "Open up...it's me, Laura."

I let my breath release slowly and my heart started to beat normally once again. I tiptoed to the window and then remembered it was nailed shut. I ran my hands under the shelf and luckily found the hammer and I pried the nail out of the window.

"Laura." I screamed in silence..

"What's up? I had to see you find out what happened, there was so much confusion on the streets." she whispered.

"Who did you talk to?" I was curious as to what people had been saying all afternoon.

"I spoke with those girls next door. They're so funny, don't you think? I mean they act like they're twins, but it's so obvious they're not."

"Oh.' I managed, then I went on, "Who else?"

"I got close enough to the cops who were working the train wreck site. Man, do they ever have a job there. Look over there, even now the gully's lit up with work lights to help out the firemen taking apart the remains of the train." she threw her head back and I could see it moving in the lit up breeze. Her golden hair glinted in the moonlight.

159

"I did mean to tell you, however..."

"Tell me what?"

"News about your cousin."

"I already know. They found her and they took her body to the morgue." I shook my head.

"Without her head attached! But you knew that already."

"Yeah. I knew, I'm the one who saw her first, although just you and I know that." I reached my arm up in pain and winced.

"What's is that? On your arms...and your face...is that blood?" she immediately pulled my arms out into the moonlight and though you could barely see, there were welt marks mixed with blood.

"*COOL!*" she said it as if it were the 'in' thing to have, not at all a beating, but a triumph! "I haven't seen marks like that since..." her voice trailed off. Then she said,

"Can you get to the bathroom to get a washcloth?"

"Not right now, my parents are still talking, I can hear them. The floor boards squeak, so I'll have to wait till after they go to sleep."

"But you haven't heard *all the new*s. I came over to give it to you straight from the horses mouth!"

"What is it?" I asked, almost too much tension was in my voice, as I practically yelled. That's when I heard my father's voice stop. I reached over and covered Laura's mouth with my fingers and gave her a quiet 'shhhh'. We waited a few minutes then I heard my Dad say, "I thought I heard something, anyway..." then I knew that it was safe to continue.

"Why are you covering my mouth?" You were the one talking so loud." Laura said, rightly so.

"I know, so what's the news you heard?"

"I heard it from that fat guy, Peter boy and Brock the

rock."

"And?"

"They said that Walter had a bloody eye and that it was swollen." she said dramatically.

"I knew that one as well."

"But I'll bet you didn't hear *how he got that way?*"

"He told me his mom did it." I said, but was anxious to hear otherwise.

"That's not how I hear it. They were talking and they said that they knew he got it in a fight. A fight that they didn't see, with a person they've never even heard of, until this afternoon."

'Ahhhhh!' I thought. "Because he got it from Margo! I went to his back door and tried to talk to him. But he had already had the swollen eye, he said his mom gave it to him for mouthing off. I'll bet Margo gave it to him right before he killed her."

162

"That was my thought, too! I'm glad we think the same." Laura said as she put her hand out to mine and gave it a gentle caress. I felt a pleasant warmth go down my throat and I nodded in agreement.

"If you believe that he killed not only your sister but your cousin as well," she said, "there's only one thing we can do about him."

"I'm thinking the same," I started, believing that we would go to the police with what we knew. But that was *not* what Laura thought.

"Good! Then we plan that we kill him, right?" Laura excitedly said.

I was shocked. I never thought about killing Walter...or did I? Goodness knows he's always been a pain to anything I tried to do, he certainly *deserved* killing.

Chapter 14

I nodded my head in agreement, then I said, "I better go. I don't want my dad to come up here and catch you."

"Right. You know something?" she asked me.

"Whats that?"

"You're sweet, and I love you!" she reached up and grabbed me by the hair, yanked it backwards and gave me a kiss, mouth closed. I was so taken by this gesture that I stood there, mouth agape, long after she left. She ran back towards the back fence in half minute, but I stood there for what seemed hours.

I fell back into my bed and immediately went to sleep. I dreamed about Nancy and Margo, my visions went lazily along until the point where they both changed into the ghosts that still haunt me today.

My nightmare started playfully enough, but when it changed it turned perverse. There they were whispering into each others ears, laughing as though they were

laughing at me-then turned and walked away. Then they

turned back around, facing me, only now they weren't the

image of 13 year old girls. Now they were the torn apart

bloody bodies as I had last seen Margo. I had never seen

the body of my sister before the funeral, but I had a good

idea of the way it was left by Walter.

I imagined she had been cut deeply through the throat,

severing the neck to the trachea. That was the way I heard

the police describe the horror scene to my mother. She

had fainted when the policeman told her this, not

thinking that there was someone in the very next room

who was listening. My stomach turned, like the time when

out family went to the amusement park and I went on

those spinning tea cups after lunch. My Dad was laughing

out loud as he told my Mom to let me eat all I wanted-it

would be funny to see the results. My lunch crawling up

my throat as the tea cups turned, watching my dad laugh at me until it came out in a splatter getting on his pants. There were saw dust shavings on the floor since I had obviously not been the first to experience the threat of the tea cups.

Dad had not wanted to appear to be the mean, obnoxious father, he smiled as he grabbed me by the arm and dragged me to the car, throwing me inside and then he yelled at me for getting puke on his pants. He locked me inside, which was a crazy thing really, when he knew I could unlock the door from the inside-but he knew I wouldn't dare. So I lay there, my head spinning with the putrid smell all over my clothes until they came back, hours later.

Then there was the ghost of Margo. She was standing with her head by her feet-fully decapitated, but smiling. Then the ghosts started to play soccer with Margo's head, which might have been the scariest things they could do, for it appeared completely innocent, as if they had not experienced death. Then they put their arms to me, they were inviting me to come play with them. I started to run, but in your dreams your feet are in permanently slow motion, so I could not run fast enough to get away from them.

Then they started to pull the skin off my body, and that's when I awoke. That's when I always woke, as I've had that dream for nearly 30 years.

The next day I woke up early, hoping to escape the house before my dad went to work. I ran through the kitchen and grabbed an apple and quietly sneaked out the back glass sliding door. I ran towards the back gate and noticed that it was open. Laura must have left it open last night. When I looked closer I saw that there were footprints, large footprints-bigger than the prints that

Laura must have left. Yes, there were her footprints, they seemed so tiny. I followed the large ones back to the house and saw that they stopped outside Jolene's window. I saw below her window a crowbar, but nothing had been opened, no window had been pried or cracked open.

Suddenly the curtains to Jolene's window opened wide and it caught my breath! It was Jolene, thank goodness.

"What are you doing out there?" she asked through the window.

I put my fingers to my lips and gestured for her to come out and see for herself. In a minute she was coming out the sliding door.

"What the hell is going on?" she demanded. I could tell she was angry, but not at me. "Your arms, your face!" she said suddenly becoming gentle. "Dad did that to you?" she looked at my arms up and down and then my face.

"You poor thing!" she almost cried. "I'm sorry that I

didn't..."

"No, no...you did the right thing. He would have beaten us both." I continued. "*This* is what I was looking at, see?" I pointed to the crowbar and I watched her fall apart.

"Oh my god...oh my god!" she cried out. "Look at the footprints, we had wiped away the old footprints, these had to be made..."

"Last night." I chimed in. "I know that Dad wouldn't have done anything. Just like the last time."

"No, I don't think he would've. We are on our own." Jolene said as she dried her tears.

"Yes, but Jolene...."

"Yeah?"

"Don't take this wrong, but I have to go. NOW!" I realized that at that moment he was calling my name, and I have to get away or face the consequences of Dad.

"Go! I'll try to cover for you." she said as she walked

169

back through the glass doors, and I immediately saw her face to face with the devil.

That was how I saw my dad in my mind. I equated him with the devil himself, and told myself that every world had it's own devil's. Some worlds more than others I have my hell, and mine had plenty. He was the kind of man that should never have had kids-only he did; it was unfortunate that it was me.

I ran towards Laura's house, going the way through the ravine. I knew it was early, maybe 6 o'clock and only the people who worked were out. I ran to the back of her house and sat there until I heard her mother's car drive away from the house. Then I ran up the door and rang the bell. Laura came out in her bathrobe and fuzzy slippers, but she was not sleepy at all, which I found strange because she had been wandering the neighborhood so late last night.

"Hey...you're up early." she said.

"Yeah, I didn't want to run into my dad. So I left about an hour ago."

"An hour? Where have you been all this time, girl?"

"Shivering in your backyard-waiting for your mom to leave." I said, "Did you run into anybody last night? Anyone in my backyard, for instance?"

"No, why?" Laura asked.

"Because there were footprints outside Jolene's window this morning, *and* a crowbar!"

"Shit!"

"Yeah, shit." I said.

"So you mean while I was wandering around last night, while I came to your window, someone else was wandering, too?"

"That's what I'm saying."

"Hell, man-that's awesome!!" I was shocked at how

haughty Laura was being. I mean, I would have been scared out of my wits. In fact, I was scared shitless by the whole affair.

"Laura," I started, "Aren't you acting a little bit..."

"A little what?"

"You're acting kind of crazy."

All of a sudden Laura's demeanor changed. She went from being friendly, to being a monster filled with rage. She grabbed my by the throat and I wrestled my way out, but not before she had cut me down the side of my face with her ragged fingernails and blood was spurting on both of us.

I ran from her house and she stood there and laughed at me. I turned back to see her lick my blood off her arm. I didn't know where to run to, home was not an option. I decided to go to Walter's house, I could see him, lighting a cigarette. I walked up to him from behind.

172

"Hey, Walter."

"What the hell do you want?"

"I'll tell you. Straight out. I think you are the murderer. I think it was you who killed my sister and my cousin." I stood up as tall as I could make myself.

"I don't know what you're talking about."

"Oh, I think you do." I said.

"Are you fucking nuts?"he said while trying to balance the cigarette precipitously in the corner of his mouth.

"What did you tell the police?"

"What police?" he asked.

"The cops that asked questions-the cops on the case of my dead sister and dead cousin!" I tried to keep my voice down, I could see my driveway and my dad's car was still there.

"I don't know what you're talking about. What do you mean your cousin, do you mean that..."he stumbled on his

173

words.

"That's right. I mean my cousin- my dear cousin was killed yesterday. Don't act like you didn't know."

"Margo...dead? That can't be." he actually looked startled.

"Don't you pretend like you didn't hear the train wreck yesterday, don't you dare!"

He stepped backwards and covered his eyes. "I did hear the train, I saw all my friends running out to the accident, but I *couldn't* see what was happening. I just *couldn't*!"

"Give me one excuse to believe you-just one!" I shouted.

"You already saw my black eye, and from your looks it doesn't matter." he said as he rubbed his hideously deformed eye.

"That's right. I don't believe the story of your mom

giving you that black eye, even though you probably deserved it. I think it was you that had Margo meet you in the ravine and that's where you lost it. It was you who went crazy and tore her head from her body!" as I finished my speech I could feel the trickles of sweat pouring down my face even though it was freezing. I had poured out my story, and now it was Walter's turn to defend himself.

"I don't know what your talking about, honest to God I don't. *Tore her head from her body?* What in the hell does that even mean?" he turned as if he were going to walk into his duplex, then he swiftly spun around to look at me with horror in his eyes.

"*YOU!* You came here blaming me, but it was you who saw her first!"

I started to feel guilty, but I had to get the truth.

"So what if I did? So what if I saw her body with her head ripped off? I didn't do it, that's why I'm here-because

I know it was you!"

"But that's why the train derailed...if her body was found decapitated, it had to be you who caused the derailment." he pointed his bony finger at me. I grabbed it and threw it down. *How dare he point his finger at me?*

"I'm going to tell the police what I know. I'm going to tell them it was you who caused the accident." he stammered as he flung himself through his door.

"Walter, Walter!" I yelled out as I hit the glass window on the back door. But he wasn't coming back.

I had to have a place to hide, I couldn't go home yet and Laura's house was not an option, so I wandered.

The day was beginning and could see people driving to work, mother's getting breakfast for their kids. I looked over into Carla and Cyndi's yard when I saw Carla letting her dog, an Alaskan malamute, Blackie, out into the yard. I ran over to her back fence and called out her name.

176

"Carla."

"Hey, stranger. What are you up to?" she said as she walked towards me, her eye's growing bigger when she noticed the belt marks on my body.

"I mouthed off to my mom." I lied. I didn't feel like going into the whole scene. "My dad hit me, no biggie."

"That's wild! Does it hurt?"

"Only when I move." I flashed a cold smile at her. She continued,

"The word on the street is that they found a body, decapitated, under the bridge. Right underneath the train."

"Oh?" I pretended like I hadn't heard. "anything else?"

"I heard that it was Margo, your cousin. But that's silly. If it was, you'd know it by now."

Her sister, Cyndi, joined us.

"Did you tell her about the gossip mill?" Cyndi couldn't get the words out fast enough.

"Yes. But I guess it wasn't who we thought it was-cause she didn't even blink when I told her."

This was too much. I couldn't take it, it had been a horrible morning, and the rest of the day wasn't turning out much better. I decided to tell the ugly stepsisters the truth so the rumors could make their way through the neighborhood and finally die down.

"Stop...just stop." I said.

"What's the matter?" they both said together.

"The stories are true. Margo was found decapitated under the bridge yesterday. These marks are from my father finding out it *was* Margo. He beat me as if it were my fault." I cried.

"That's awful!" they both chimed. "Surely he couldn't think you had anything to do with it."

"If something bad were to happen to one of us, Mom and Dad would think it was the other's fault. Like I'm

178

your keeper?" Cyndi said nodding her head, Carla joined in.

"Do you want to come in awhile? At least until your dad leaves for work." They both invited me in, and I accepted.

Later we were up in their room, they had a two story house with a basement which I thought resembled a mansion. I felt safe there. We managed to get into their second story room without having to see anyone, but I could hear the voices of their parents calmly chatting below.

I had always thought that it was a myth, the classic family as portrayed on television. Every week we would tune into the family dramas and comedies, and every week you could see warmth and caring in their eyes. You could see love. Love was a staple that I had not yet experienced. I often would think what happened in the life of my

Mother to make her think that marrying my Dad would be a *good* idea. Surely he didn't become this monster, he must have shown signs of being an angry drunk and wife beater *way* before they got married. Even after they married, there must have been times when she could have left him- if not for herself, *for us*. I couldn't imagine living on welfare being worse. I had decided long ago that I would never put a loved one in that situation, because I was going to finish school and become someone, anyone...

...and never, ever count on a man.

It was Carla's voice that brought me back to the present.

"Besides the unspeakable thing that happened to Margo yesterday, we have heard more rumors."

"Umm?" I asked.

"It seems that there was a big guy that came to Walter's house." Carla said.

"Yeah. Not only did he come to his house, he *beat* Walter within an inch of his life!" Cyndi continued.

"How do you know this?"

"Yesterday...in the crowds...we *saw* him!" Carla said.

"You both- you saw him? You saw a strange man? How do you know who he was?"

"We heard him talking to one of Walter's friends, Peter boy-the chunky one." Cyndi said.

"And we heard him tell Peter boy that he had come from Walter's duplex where he took care of some business, all the while he's p-punching his hand." Carla followed.

"I don't understand."

"Don't you see? By 'taking care of business' he meant that he beat up Walter." the girls looked at each other with a nod.

"How can you know this?" I asked as they smiled. "I mean I know he had to be elsewhere at the time."

"You can't deny the timing-this was while the crowds were forming from the train accident. No, we're sure."

I thought for a moment. This was *not* good news. I thought I had it all down to the minute. Walter was the *one*. Now they were putting my timeline in danger.

"Do me a favor, will you?" I asked Carla.

She nodded her head.

"Please see if my dad's car is gone. I do not want to run into him today."

Carla walked to the window, then back to me. "He's gone."

"Okay. Thank you for letting me hide here. See ya." I said as I ran out the door. I could hear them run down to tell their parents about how their rumors were true. Especially the one about Margo. But I did not care. I ran straight to my room and closed the door. I jumped onto my bed and pulled the pillow down over my face

and fell back to sleep.

Chapter 15

The following Monday it was time to go back to vacation Bible school. I was 5 minutes late, but when I arrived nobody seemed to want to talk to me. Even more than usual. It's as if I had become invisible-*Poof!* No one would even sit near me in the circle on the floor.

Laura was there, just smiling this huge Cheshire cat grin. When Bill finally let us go for the day he asked me to stay awhile-he wanted to *wrap*. When all the kids had left he began, "This is hard, I never thought I would have to kick anyone out of here."

'What? Kicked out of here? Are you joking?" the shock was overwhelming. I had never been kicked out of anything before, let alone a Bible school! At first I thought it was because of Nancy and Margo-that maybe I was making some of the others uncomfortable just by being there. I had to ask.

"Why are you kicking me out? Is it because of Nancy and Margo?"

"NO. That's *NOT* the reason. I wouldn't even know how to tell you-it's just that *we* don't want *your* kind coming to this church ever again." Bill looked confused, but certainly not as much as I was.

"I don't know what you mean, *my kind?* I'm just like the other kids- I'm just a kid." I pleaded.

"No, you're not. You're *different*. I don't know how to make it clearer than that. We don't want you to come here-ever again-never!" Bill mumbled something else that I could not make out, then he picked up his stuff and escorted me out before he locked the door.

I had started crying by then but I saw through my tears Laura, who was staring at me at the edge of the parking lot-and smiling, just before she turn and ran.

Chapter 16

My dreams were the same as they had been before, dreams of Nancy and Margo turning into scary creatures of the night. It was late afternoon then I heard the door slam from the other room, my dad was home. I could tell he had been drinking and I wanted to get out of the house by any means possible. I opened my window to climb out when I heard, "Surprise!" It was Laura.

"Come on." she whispered.

I kicked out the screen and followed her out of the yard. When we were in the alley and I knew we were safe, I confronted her.

"What in the hell were you doing outside my window? Didn't you get enough blood before? And what the hell was Bill talking about at Bible school? Do you know that I can't ever *go* to that church again? I don't know what I'm going to tell my mother when she tries to get me up for church on Sunday. "

"I was playing a joke on you. Bad timing, I know. But you can't still be mad about it, can you?"

"A joke? You scratched my face until it bled!" I yelled at her.

"Too bad, so sad. Are you going to join me, or not?"

"Join you for what?" I couldn't understand what she was talking about.

"Killing Walter." I think she was joking, surely she couldn't mean that.

"I'm not 100% sure it was Walter." I said.

"Not 100% sure? What do you need- a signed confession? What kind of pussy are you?" she said as she picked up a ball of mud and smeared it on my face.

I fell back.

"What was that for?" I asked.

"It was for luck. That's what we used to do for luck in a case like this."

"Smearing my face with mud?" I was puzzled.

"That's right, girl. It has something to do with feeding the trolls before we start to unearth the hungry devils. It's a tradition., for good luck." she said, "Now you do it to me, go ahead."

Then she stood there waiting for me to smear her face with mud. I did so, but it felt so wrong. She put her pinky finger in my face waiting for me to put my pinky with hers in a kind of mutual alliance. Again, I did what she wanted, but somehow the whole day seemed askew.

"Ok," she announced, "now we are in agreement, correct?"

"About what?"

"On our plan to kill Walter, but first I wanted to take you on a little trip." she was grinning like she was mad.

188

"What?" I said, then, "Where?"

"We're going to the asylum!" she grabbed my elbow and pulled me along with incredible strength. "Come on."

"Wait!" I shouted. "What makes you think I even want to go to the asylum? I mean until recently I didn't even know that this place existed, now you want to actually go to the asylum?"

"Well sure. Of course I do-why wouldn't you want to go with me?" she asked me while her mad smile turned into a frown.

"It's not that I don't want to follow you..."

"Great! Let's go."

"How would you know where this asylum is located? How do I know you're not leading me on a wild goose chase?" I asked.

"I've been there before." she answered.

"*You've been there?*" I was astonished. *How in the*

world?

"Yes, I have. Remember my mom is a nurse?"

I nodded.

"Well she's taken me there, before it closed. She thought it would be good for me to see a real asylum, instead of reading about them in a book." she explained.

"So you know about asylums? Maybe you could give me a lesson while we walk- I'm very interested. I've heard stories..."

"I'll bet you have."

"How sure are you that we can even get inside? Isn't it closed, like fenced in?" I asked.

"Oh, we're not going to get in through the front door. We'll go in the way the community gets in."

"What community?" I asked her as we walked westward.

It was late afternoon, the sun had not yet set because

of the time of year. I didn't even have a sweater because the weather had been so beautiful. I smiled towards the sun, letting the rays bathe me as we walked. I couldn't help but think about how terrible the last few weeks had been, but the whole time the weather had been so sublime.

"The 'Community' is what the people who lived there call themselves now that they're living on the streets." she explained.

"Laura," I asked suspiciously, "How would you know that?"

"I hear things, you know, I've asked my mom. She knows all about that place."

"I remember. You told me. She worked there, right?"

"Oh yeah, I forgot that I told you that." she said absentmindedly.

There was another thing- where was her accent? The morning of the accident she all southern draws

191

and Texas talk. Now she was talking normally. She had even called me 'girl' when I had approached before. We continued to walk west as her accent was more of a girl from around the corner, and not from Texas at all.

She went on and on about the architect who designed the buildings after a castle in England, and even imported the ceiling tiles from a library that was being deconstructed in Surrey for the library in the main house. How he was a madman himself, but a genius madman who never wrote down his ideas and blueprints, but kept them inside his brilliant mind. But how it turned into disaster after the death of this man halfway through construction.

"He hung himself, people say that his spirits roam the halls, or some shit like that. That's why I say it's haunted instead of cursed."

"But people say it's cursed because of the tragedies

that happened here, I haven't heard of his spirit being here." I said somewhat confused.

"Well there you go-they're only stories after all. It was built in 1850 or thereabouts, when Colorado wasn't even a state-it was the Kansas territory. They never thought Denver would take off like it did, but it *did* take off and ended up being here in the suburbs, in Lakewood."

We continued to walk for almost two miles, as the sun made it's way to the top of the mountains.

"There it is!" she said with an excitement in her voice.

She pointed to a vine covered crumbling wall that must have been 12 feet high. There was now a fence in front of the entrance with large red letters that read *Keep Out!* In various languages. When we arrived at the front fence we could see where there was a huge padlock pretending to keep people out, but it was obvious that it was for naught. We peeked inside and we could see inside

193

to the red brick colored, almost medieval looking buildings, falling apart in some places, covering acres of land that stretched further than your eye could see.

Standing there looking in, it seemed as though I was standing in another world. I had stepped from Lakewood into the next dimension. Laura held out her hand and started to walk me around the acres once held as an asylum, to the back where holes gaping behind the bushes, on the other side of the chain link fence and crumbling stone wall, standing guard to the fortress. We walked to where there was a opening that looked like someone had torn the metal open, past the chain link, past the razor wire. The monstrous wall looked inadequate where it once stood mighty and imposing, and now all that was left were wild bushes standing tall, but were hardly enough to keep out even a child.

"Come on. No one can see us." Laura said.

"Are you sure we won't get caught?"

"No way." she said, then she started running through the bushes and gnarled trees past the medieval buildings towards the entrance of the sewer, and disappeared straight under the heavy metal lid. I looked down the massive tunnel and could barely see anything but the questionable ladder she was climbing down. I started to follow her and my hands were getting slimy from the crud that seemed to be lining the cave. I heard her 'plop' down and I knew I was close behind. When I was on level with Laura I said,

"What the hell is this place?" I was astonished that she led me here. "I thought we were going to the asylum."

"Hold your horses. Were almost there." She looked in the backpack she had brought and took out a flashlight and illuminated the tunnel we had entered. There was a layer of water at my feet and a definite sound of liquid being sloshed around. It was dark with only a piercing of light from Laura's flashlight. I could tell that we were walking towards the asylum, at least in the general direction of the main building. The tunnels were imposing, and led to thousands of miles in each direction. Yes, I was going to keep up with Laura, for I did not want to lose my way down in the putrid sewers. The smell was repugnant for I had never had such an odor assault my nostrils like this before. I frowned deeply and started breathing through my mouth instead of my nose and found some relief.

"Where do these tunnels go? Are they going to all the buildings?" I asked.

"Yes. Now be quiet, the walls here act like a loudspeaker, you can hear people from a mile away if you tried." She whispered.

When we finally arrived at the ladder to which I believe was the main building I asked if we were going

196

to the library, the place I really wanted to see.

"No. Were going to go up the ladder in the 'C' compound, that's where they had the craziest people locked up."

"What? You never said anything about C compound before! I wanted to see the building itself, the *main* building." I stammered. "I wanted to see the library ceiling you told me about."

"Oh, you are such a crybaby!" She took my hand and pulled me along the sewer until we reached the ladder for the C compound. I was scared to death. She started to climb and I followed, partly because I was terrified of being left alone in the darkness.

When I heard the scraping of the sewer cover and the brightness which engulfed us, I knew we were there. It was not quite like I expected when I climbed out of the hole, it wasn't like a hospital setting, it was more of a medieval torture chamber. There were rusty metal cuffs chained to the walls, and rows of cells meant for single use but it was evident that there were many held in the space for one. The smell was hideous, even while empty. There were yellow stains on the walls, ceilings and floors – I knew what they were from, you could not help knowing that they were from when you got a whiff that smelled like cat pee.

There was also an overpowering smell that came from the piles brown excrement. I could not help but ask her… "Why have you brought me here?"

"Because I wanted to introduce you to some of the people that live here."

"But *no one* lives here!" I demanded, "you even said that the place was closed down for good!"

"That's what we *tell* people. The truth is that many of the inmates didn't have any place to go, some of them

198

broke back in and have reclaimed their old buildings and cells. Of course they don't have beds and linens now like the used to, but they manage all right."

I couldn't believe my ears.

"But there's no electricity! I know it gets cold in the fall, colder even in the winter! How do they..."

"Eat, sleep, use the bathroom?" She said.

"Yes!" I exploded.

"They manage. Now come on." Again she yanked my elbow and turn the corner, I couldn't believe my eyes.

There, in all their glory were the wretched, thrown away miscreants, thrown around the small rooms eating the tidbits of food they had picked out of the garbage landfills during the day. There was a broken old man dressed in tatters who had a small grill, and which he was warming and icky looking soup of goo. He was taking a sip when he looked up and saw us, or me rather than since he apparently knew Laura.

"Who is the pretty little lady?" He asked Laura.

"No one. Don't pay attention to him, he's trying to be charming." She told me.

I was *not* flattered by his soothing ways and gladly ignored him as we continue to walk around the corners.

"You *know* these people?"

"Sure I do. I used to live with them, before the shutdown." She said casually.

"*You lived here?*" I was shocked by her admission. I expected her to answer me, but she did not and continued.

"Laura!" I exclaimed, "STOP!" I screamed. I grabbed her arm but she threw it away and suddenly screamed at me, "What in the hell is wrong with you?"

"Wrong with *me?*" I answered back, "I think you have some explaining to do."

We stared each other down, both thinking we were right, at least that's what I've come to believe over the years. I thought she owed me the explanation as to her being an inmate at so young an age, and what we were doing here. I believe she was thinking she was right for carrying her deep-seated anger around, and coming up with the plan to kill Walter. She did have a point, and that's where I faltered in judgment. I wanted to believe her.

"Just tell me," I said, "everything."

Chapter 17

"Alright. I guess you deserve that much." She said, "get ready for your education- I have a lot to tell you."

"Okay." I said as I noticed where we had stopped. It was eerily twilight, and this hallway seemed to be caught in the middle between daylight and evening. There were clouds that were laying low, making it seem as if we were in a movie about vampires. But there were no *Dark Shadows*, there where no vampires, we were, however, surrounded by madmen.

The hallway was long and narrow, and I could imagine in my mind the days when it would be filled with screaming, insane lunatics wrapped up in their white straitjackets and the tall, strong orderlies also dressed in white leading them from room to room.

"First of all, I *was* an inmate here for several years. The judge ruled that I was too young to be sent to prison, but too old to be set free. He sent me here to live out my days till I turned 21." Laura said.

I had a huge lump in my throat but I had to ask, "why were you an inmate, Laura?"

"Because I killed a man. I wanted to kill him, he deserved it." Laura said.

"Why?"

"Because he had been abusing me for years. He was the boyfriend of my goody-two-shoes mom. He had been living with us because he was a child molester but Mom just couldn't see it. When I first told her about what he was doing she said that I was making it up. As time went by she said that I was 'coming on' to him, so even if he was molesting me, it was my fault!" Her breathing started getting faster, I could tell it was hard for her to tell me more. But she did.

"I told her that if he kept coming in my room at

night to molest me, I would do something that would make him sorry. Boy did I make him sorry." Her eyes glazed.

"There's this kind of knife that you can't get just anywhere, you know what I mean?"

I shook my head no. I did not know what she meant.

"It's the kind of knife that fits between your fingers, like brass knuckles that have serrated edges. You can punch out a person and really be knifing them at the same time. Well, it took me a long time to get the knives, one for each hand, but when I got them I waited. I didn't have to wait too long either. He came to me with this stinking breath all over my neck and he was groping me, and I let him have it." Laura said with a smile. She terrified me, she continued.

"That night when he crawled into bed with me, he

had this nasty smile on his face when I turned towards him, but I wiped it off fast. I gave him one slice across the face and one punch in the gut. He started to scream, so I started to slice faster, I wanted him to feel the pain I had felt before he died. He was still alive, just a little, when my mom came running into the room. She ran to him, can you believe it? *She went to him!* Of course he died, I planted my strikes precisely. Somehow she managed to call the police, and an ambulance – but it was no use, he died before the ambulance came. The policeman came into my room with a gun on me – *on me!* I put down the knives without incident. I wasn't a threat to anybody else, except him. I didn't cry, I didn't do whatever they thought I should have done, so they put me into an insane asylum." Her face looked like she was a million miles away, she went on, "so I lived here, for decades it seemed, but it couldn't be – could it? I'm only 14. *I'm only 14!* But then the announcement came that they were closing the asylum. My mom *acted* like the good mother then – Ha! She petitioned the court, talked them into letting me stay with her. She thinks that she can control me after spending *years* in that pit. She was too late. I was raped so many times, sometimes by the guards, sometimes by the inmates. The guards had quite a little racket going on, *'Have sex with the youngest inmate we've ever had – only a packet of cigarettes!' Sometimes it was twice a night, which might not sound like a lot to you but those nights it would keep me awake, screaming into the night. But then the screaming stopped. And it got to be routine, I stopped feeling anything. Then it just cut into my sleep – and I would be groggy the next day."*

I was petrified. *It might not sound like a lot to you?* Being raped once sounded like a lot to me, let alone the hundreds, maybe even thousands of times she had it done to her. I sat where I had once stood.

"My mother didn't believe me, *again!* She let me stay in this prison for years. Probably making me pay for killing her precious boyfriend. When she finally did get me home, she was the same old whore of a mother once more. She goes out almost every night, sometime she had her boyfriends come home with her. That's when I can hear both of them, sometimes three of them, – *it's disgusting!"* She sat down beside me.

"How long have you been out?" I asked.

"Since it closed last year. I lied to you when I told you she was a nurse here. I lied when I told you she *was* a nurse period. I was making it up. I made up Texas. I know I told you I came from Texas, but that was part of my lie as well. It sounded *exotic.* She works in a sleazy bar on Colfax. That's where she picks up the foul men she meets." She patted my hand and left it. I started to feel the warmth of her hand, it was seeping into the frigid cold of my fingers.

"I'm sorry. For everything that's happened to you, *really I am*."

"There's one other thing..." she said as she looked at me, petrified as to what I might think. That's rich! Nothing she told me now would shock me, then she continued.

"I had a child."

Chapter 18

I guess I was wrong, she did shock me. "What the? Are you shitting me?" I gasped.

"I had a child! Don't you believe me either?" her cheeks suddenly getting flushed.

"What do you mean, either? You can't tell me *nobody* believed you-surely someone had to know." I said my mouth getting dry, I realized that I hadn't had anything to drink on the whole trip, now I was feeling arid.

"Yeah, they knew. The whole staff knew as did the other inmates. No one would say anything about it-playing dumb- maybe it would go away."

"But your mom, she had to know. Didn't she get you help?" I was dumbfounded.

"Her way of helping? By NOT helping! She didn't want to believe me anymore than the staff did-they were all in the big secret, every damn one of them!" She fell on her knees, hitting hard the concrete on the cold stone floor.

"I remember when *it* happened. I was about 7 months pregnant, I couldn't tell for sure who's baby it was- it could have been anyone's baby, let alone *when* I got pregnant. I was locked up in solitary, I don't know why but the guards thought someone might tell-they needn't have bothered. It was the middle of the night when the pains started, I began screaming for help, but no one came. It got worse and worse and I thought I was going to die-but God's not that kind. There was blood all over the walls all over me, but the contractions continued. I tried to hit my swollen belly, tried to make the monster inside me come out. I felt like I was being split in two, when suddenly I pulled the thing out-it was a boy." she face was red from crying. Now, she looked at me and I could tell that she had genuine feelings for her baby.

"A beautiful baby boy, I loved him immediately. As I held his little body I expelled the placenta, only now I couldn't feel the pain. I grabbed him and held him close, and I felt him cry, it was so life-changing! I was a mother! I was a god-damned mother. I felt the warm rush of love that I had never known before, never even knew about before. I just lay there rocking back and forth, holding my crying baby."

I started to cry myself. I knew something was foreboding, something terrible.

"Then...then.." she was trying to talk, but her mouth was slobbery. She continued after a moment. "The guards unlocked the doors, and came into the room. I'll never forget their faces...*not ever!!* They looked at me with their pale and dirty incoherent faces and they took him."

"What? Where? Where did they take him?" I said, my mouth becoming parched.

"I don't know! Honestly, I don't know. They pushed me back into the room and locked me up again. I screamed until I became horse, and when they finally did let me out they told me that he quit breathing almost as quickly as they closed my door. I wouldn't let it go-I accused them of selling the baby and splitting the money between them. I told my doctor and they told him that I had a psychotic episode, that I had to be strapped down to my bed. That my bleeding was from banging my head on the floor, cutting myself against the bed-so what choice did they have?" she said, calming down now as her story was ending. "The guards told me that they could prove to me that my baby was dead. They walked me out to the cemetery; me in a straight jacket being led one guard on each side, to a small mound, no headstone. They told me that's where they buried him. I started screaming for them to let me out of the straight jacket, but they wouldn't unlock the arms. I fell on the mound and started to get mouthfuls of dirt, trying to dig his body up. But they pulled me away, and I never did get to see if their story was true. Maybe I'll get another chance." she said as she got up and took me against the wall.

She squeezed my thumb, lifted my hand and put it behind her shoulder. She kissed me, and I let her. It felt tingly and wonderful. She stood up and announced,

"Let's go. There are some people I want you to meet." I blindly followed her.

When we arrived where the human sewage smelled the worst, there was a young man who looked half like he was from the street and half like he was completely comfortable in his insane surroundings. Laura introduced us, his name was Vincent. He seemed to be perfectly normal, but I realized I was in no normal place. Laura whispered in his ear and he laughed.

"Laura," he said, "haven't you had enough of those?"

"Those, what?" I asked.

Vincent put his finger on my mouth, wanting me to be silent.

"You'll find out, soon enough." He laughed again, this time he had a crazy laugh, I thought, *that's what I've been expecting!*

He left the darkening the room for a moment, and that's when I saw people around me. An old lady who was dressed in shreds touched my hair and I jumped.

"Hair, so pretty! I just want to burn it. Please let me burn it." I grabbed my hair and shouted, "NO!"

"Don't be afraid of her, she wants to burn everyone's hair. Go away, Myra! Shoo!" Laura said.

Vincent came back into the room carrying a black sack. He held it out to Laura and she said with a quick,

214

"Thanks. Your a gem." She put the bag into the backpack that she carried in, and we started to walk out.

I could feel the stares going right through me from the motley bunch of lunatics. I could hear their mumbles, mostly to themselves, and it broke my heart.

"Are we going to leave, just like that?" I asked.

"Just like what? We can't do anything for them, they are insane. Short of paying for hospital care, there's nothing we can do."

"I guess you're right." I sadly admitted.

I could see the asylum grounds as the light went over the mountains. The sky was a brilliant salmon color. How a mid-evil broken down series of buildings could look so beautiful and disturbing at the same time was beyond me. The grass was brown now, no longer fed the water it needs to stay alive, and full of weeds now that there was no one to care for the once manicured lawns.

215

There were patches of old tattered clippings that filled the spaces between the old edifices. From the broken windows there wasn't a sound that came out the buildings, they were eerily quiet. No one would ever even know about the life that went on inside the invisible hiding spots, cradled inside the facade.

There was one spot that was not compound 'c', or any compound for that matter. It was the broken down cemetery across the fields. It looked so wretched, pieces of headstones left there in the desolation. I pulled Laura's arm and went into the abandoned graveyard and saw that the headstones were merely a convenience, for they had the numbers of the dead inmates, not the names. I asked Laura about this curiosity.

"Why do they have numbers? Couldn't they even put the names on the stones? Couldn't they give them that much dignity?" I said as my face slackened.

"No. That's all the respect they got. We were numbers on a piece of paper, inmate number 1000, 1001, 1002...just numbers."

"So these are the people who didn't have the relatives to come and claim their bodies?"

"Yes. This is where they ended up. Sad, huh?" Laura actually looked grief stricken.

"I'm feeling very spooked right now. We better go."

"Why? Because of the pathetic losers whose graves we're standing on?" she said as she flipped her hair to one side. Her grief was no where to be seen. It was weird, one minute she was grief stricken, the next, she was fine. Her mood swings were beginning to scare me.

"Yes. Let's go." I said as I started backing my way out of the cemetery. I was afraid to turn my back on the dead.

"Wait a minute. I have to do this." she said as she walked between the headstones to a small mound of dirt. I

217

knew what she was doing. I stood and watched.

Laura began to tear at the dirt with a fury, not knowing what she was going to find. When she finally came to a small sack she lifted it and started a heart-wrenching cry. She held the bag to her heart and then started to open it's drawstring top. I yelled at her to stop, I surely did *not* want to see it's contents. But she did open the bag, and her crying became sobs.

"Look, there's a guards rag stuffed in his mouth, see here? There's the asylums symbol. He *was alive* when they buried him...he was alive."

She hugged it once more, then put it into her backpack with the bag she had gotten from Vincent. it seemed not to matter to her that they were all intermingling, she didn't care.

When we ran across the fields to the sewer where we went out of the asylum I stopped her before we went down.

"Laura, please tell me what it is we came here for."

"All right!" She said smiling again, "we came for these." As she pulled out a couple of knives from her bag. Not ordinary knives, but the knives she had told about to cut up her mother's boyfriend.

"What do we need these for? I mean it, Laura – what the hell?"

"We need these knives to kill Walter! We can't be sure of his death unless we both attack him with an assault of weapons, these knives." She shook as she said this, and I looked at the knives – they had old blood stains on them. And I wasn't even absolutely that it *was* Walter. Especially after this friendly fire visit to the asylum.

"I don't think it was Walter, not for sure, anyway."

"But he killed your sister and your cousin, you'd be a *hero* for killing the bastard!"

219

I was young, too young to realize that a psychotic person would make up stories like being a hero, she *sounded* sane.

"Okay, you're right. So, how do we do this? One for me and one for you?"

"That's right. But we have to find a way to get Walter out of his house and down into the ravine. That way no one will ever know it was us, because the ravine already has blood from two murderers! So one more won't matter." She said as she walked into the sewer with me following close behind.

We were back into the sewers again. Once more the smell was grievous to my nose and once again I started breathing out my mouth. It seemed like we walked through miles of the sewer system, making twists and turns, but Laura knew her way around the stinking cesspool when we came upon a man with crazy hair, sleeping in the shit of the sewer. He frightened me, I'm not afraid to admit it. He looked familiar, then I realized it was the gully tramp who chased us and who's face I had kicked. But I walked past him, trying to ignore him. Laura finally made her way through miles of tunnels and up the ladder, and I was stunned! When she opened the sewer lid and I climbed out I was in a daze-she had come out into the ravine, to the old sewer lid I had recently discovered. *This can't be*, I thought, *This can't be happening, there is something incredibly odd with the whole fiendish scheme!*

"Laura," I muttered, "do you know where we are? Why didn't you tell me that you knew about this sewer the whole time?"

"I never said I did or *didn't* know. It was you who was surprised by the presence of the manhole cover-not I."

"Believe me, I know there's not a whole lot that I

didn't know before tonight! But one thing is for sure, like I told you, I'm not even sure about Walter's guilt-too many things that don't add up. The Charbonneau girls told me about a man who was at Walters earlier and they put him there just as the train derailed-the time doesn't add up!"

Laura looked at me like a wounded puppy, with her turning her lips into a pucker. Then she said,

"This is where I leave you." She said as she pressed her lips on my cheek. "I'll check back with you around midnight, so be awake."

I touched my cheek and felt that tingle once again. I mumbled, "Uh huh." And she left me disappearing down the alley. I knew I couldn't walk in the doorway, my Dad was home again so I sneaked back into my window. I stayed there in the dark, hoping that neither my Mom or Dad would bother to check in, thinking instead that I was staying at the neighbor's house.

Finally around 10 PM I heard my folks turn into bed. I could hear the faint music coming from Jolene's room and I thought it might be safe to visit her.

When I got there I quietly tapped on her door, when she opened the door she looked shocked.

"What are you doing here? I thought you were staying with Carla and Cyndi!"

"Shhhhh." I whispered, "that's what I wanted you to think. I've been in my room waiting for Mom and Dad to go to sleep."

"Get in here." She said as she closed her door. "Where have you been all day? I was starting to get worried."

"Thanks for that. I'm afraid that you would be the only one worried if I went missing."

"That's not true. You're wrong."

"I wanted to tell you that I love you, in case

223

anything happens tonight." I said with sincerity.

"What?" Jolene looked at me strangely. "Why would you say that? What happens tonight?"

"I'm going out." That's all I could say, "I may be back by morning, I may not. I love you. I just wanted you to know how I feel. I've never sincerely said *I love you* to anybody before, not even Mom. But I wanted you to know how I feel."

Jolene grabbed my shoulders, and the next minute she was hugging me.

"I love you too, you little shit." She had tears in her eyes. "Do me a favor and don't go out tonight."

"I have to. I need to. This is for Nancy and Margo."

"Then tell me where you'll be." She was trying to get the location out of me, but it wasn't going to work.

"I can't. I'm going to my room now. Good night." I

224

turned in tiptoed out, shutting my door as quietly as possible behind me. I stayed in the dark until the hour came when I heard a tapping at my window. It was Laura. Slowly I opened my window and crept out. We ran across the yard out to the back of Walter's window.

"Remember, say whatever you have to to get him to come out." Laura said.

I wasn't sure exactly what I should say, but I tried my best. I knocked three times. He came to the window and opened it wide.

"What the hell do you want?" he bellowed.

"I wanted to say I'm sorry. I wanted to say it in the moonlight where your friends couldn't see us."

Laura was hiding in the bushes around the corner, but she could hear all that was said. She started motioning me to get him to the ravine.

"You said it, now go. I don't want to talk to you

anymore." Walter said.

"Please! All I want is to talk to you in more detail about what happened. I know it wasn't you who killed them. *Please?* I have an idea who it was, and you'll want to know." I pleaded and made *my* puppy face. It worked.

"All right. I'll meet you out back."

"NO! No. Let's meet in the gully, under the bridge."

"Why would you want to meet there?"

"I just do. Come on!" I waved him over and took off for the bridge, in the darkness of the over-passing cloud, he couldn't see Laura run ahead. He also couldn't see she carried a bag with the knives. I started to get tense and couldn't find relief for what I was feeling.

I joined Laura under the bridge in the moonlight and such moonlight it was! It was the brightest I've seen the moon in ages. The moon cast a shadow and it was no problem seeing where he was going. We could see Walter coming down the hill and Laura said,

"Here, take this!" It was one of the knives she was carrying. I slipped my fingers between the sheaves and hid my hand behind my back. Laura hid on the outside of the bridge opposite to the hill Walter came down.

"Silence!" Laura whispered, "When I give you the sign we knife him, okay?"

"Are you sure, Laura?" I started to ask, but Walter soon joined us.

"Okay. What did you want to tell me?"

"You already know. I wanted to say I am sorry for accusing you of murder. It was a shitty thing to do, and I wanted to tell you in private."

"So Margo told you what happened before Nancy died, huh?" Walter said.

"What are you talking about?"

"She must have told you, only you were in so much pain that it took a few days to let it sink in, right?"

"Walter," I said, "told me what, exactly?"

"The day that Nancy died, I met the two of them down here."

"*That* I know. "

"Margo started teasing me and Nancy came to my defense." He mumbled.

"I figured that." I said.

"Margo could feel that there was something going on between Nancy and me, and she left. After she left I started to kiss Nancy, and she started to kiss me back." He turned his back to me.

"All I wanted was a blow job, that's all! I've been hearing about these from the other guys, like Peter boy, and so I asked her if she wouldn't mind giving me one."

"And that's when she turned you down and you got

228

so mad that you killed her, right?" I could feel my hand with the knife's clenching.

"NO! She gave me one. I swear! It felt so good, and I told her that. Then she said that she would have to fix herself up and so I left – honest. I met Margo up the hill and she asked me about what happened, so I told her. She seemed so cool with it. So cool that I pulled her behind the big tree at the top of the hill and started making out with her, too! I got up her shirt and then I could hear Peter boy and Nick coming so I ran off with them. Then I went home and watched TV. The next thing I knew everyone was in the gully talking about a murder that it had just taken place. Margo and I looked for Nancy, but only for a minute. Margo believed me, she believed me! She promised me that she would keep it secret, what happened between Nancy and her and me." He was almost in tears. "Then I saw her talking to you that day the train crashed. She saw me looking at her through the window and I guess she panicked. She ran away."

I was furious! *How dare you take my sister's name in vain!*

"You lie! You're a liar." I screamed.

Just then Laura came out of hiding and she jumped on top of Walter and stabbed him in the gut, while holding him down with her knees. The most gruesome sound came out of Walter, and he tried desperately to get away. He was crying like a small child-helpless.

"Come on! You have to stab him too." She screamed.

Walter tried to crawl away, stumbling on his hands and feet. Blood was ooozing from his body-I could see it in the moonlight. It only took a few moments. But that was enough.

I ran after him, and stabbed him in the back. Laura

joined me and we took turns stabbing him over and over again. He fell at the bottom of the hill, letting out a heart wrenching wail. Laura stood up with her knives shining red in the moonlight and said, "that was *so awesome*!" She was out of breath, "I wish he would stand up so I could stab him again." She said with her voice dripping with hatred.

"Laura, did you hear what he said about Nancy?" I asked.

"Yeah, I heard him. What a sick bastard."

"You don't think he was telling the truth, do you?" I had an awful feeling in the pit of my stomach.

Could it be he was telling me the truth about my little sister? But no. He couldn't have told me the truth, because I just took place in *his* murder! I let the knives fall from between my fingers and held them out to Laura.

"Here, you better take these. I better get back to the

231

house and get some sleep, or at least try to pretend I can sleep. I don't think I actually can." She put the knives back in her black bag and patted me on the back.

"Good job. Great job, actually." Then she took me by the back of my head and drew me close to her, I could feel her breath. Then she gave me the longest kiss yet, my knees were giving way as the warmth travel down my spine. This was all too much! She was kissing me as we stood over Walter's dying body. Then the kiss ended, and she said,

"Yes, you better get home. I'll come by tomorrow, okay?"

"Okay." I said halfheartedly, as part of me was still floating. I felt very weak now as I started to walk back to our house, my throat was completely parched.

I did not understand what was going on, partly. Then part of me understood completely. Of course she was coming on to me, because she had been raped repeatedly

by men; girls seemed safe to her, *I* seemed safe to her. It

was only because passion was new to me, passion from

man or woman, that I was falling into her fantasy. There

was a part of me that wanted that fantasy to continue, but

a bigger part wanted me to play out the fantasy with a

boy, or man.

I walked back up the alley and slid through my

window and shut it tight. I fell asleep until the morning

when I heard a chilling scream. Surely it was Jolene? I

heard the footsteps run up the stairs and my mom and dad

and I all ran into Jolene's room at the same time. There,

underneath the open window was a broken curtain rod

above Jolene's head. The breeze was blowing through the

broken window and there was blood everywhere, and

Jolene barely had a breath left in her as the knife lay close

by her. Outside her room there was the body of a man who

tried to come in last night, but found a ready and willing Jolene, prepared to protect herself.

I jumped over Jolene's barely breathing body and yelled, "Get an ambulance! Quick! She's alive, but not if you don't get an ambulance here soon."

My mother saw her and started crying uncontrollably, while my dad ran to the phone to call for help. I immediately started tearing her blankets into long strips and began to bandage her head, which was bleeding the most. She motioned me with her finger.

"I'm okay. Really. How do you think I managed to scream?" Then she started to weekly laugh. "I think I got him, didn't I?"

"Don't talk, my sweet sister." I said, "you got him, though. You got him."

Chapter 19

The police came and ambulance as well, Jolene went with them to the hospital, and of course the man who tried to kill her was dead in the backyard. Jolene had kept a knife in bed with her ever since we had found footprints leading to her window two nights ago. She was ready for him, all right.

The police took as much information from her as they could before the ambulance driver insisted on taking her to the hospital where the doctor would give them permission on questioning her more. But here's what I heard her say: that the man had come back and let himself into *my* window, and when he found no one in that room he must have crept into the bedroom next door. Jolene must have heard him and thought it was me so she made no sudden moves until he was on top of her using his own knife to chop her up. Jolene wrestled with the man for a

235

moment, she got the knife and thrust it into his back, he tried to get away but she must have hit a hidden artery because he bled to death right outside of her window. She remembered passing out and felt weak and she thought she was going to die she must have had mostly flesh wounds because she woke up and began screaming when she remembered what happened. That's the scream when we all found her bleeding on the floor, and him lying in the backyard, dead.

The policeman who was talking to Jolene was the same man we had talked to before, in the ravine, Mitch's older brother. He wanted to make sure Jolene was alive and well. He said that this was the man they had been looking for he was the murderer.

But he couldn't be the murder! The real murderer was dead in the hollow as we spoke, it had to be Walter!

"Yessiree." The cop said, "we always thought it

was an inmate from the old asylum, and now we have proof!"

"What kind of proof?" I asked him quivering.

"On his left wrist, you can see it from here." He walked over to the window and pointed out where cops were all over the place, measuring footprints, taking pictures and getting blood samples.

"There is a tattoo, a number. That's the way they kept track of the criminally insane prisoners. That's who we were looking for. His name was Cromwell." He said with a certain satisfaction.

"Yeah, he did this – but how can you be sure he killed my little sister and cousin?" I nervously replied.

"These people always leave tracks, their mark if you will. I'll bet that the skin samples we got from underneath the girls fingernails will match right up with his. And see there? His fingernails are still dirty, probably

237

hasn't washed them for weeks. I'll bet that the girls tissue samples are under there. Yup, we got our man."

I started to shake and fell on my knees. The policeman thought it was due to finding Jolene – how could I tell him it wasn't from finding her, but it was because I had killed a man, a mere boy, for the murders? I remember he sat me down on the couch in the living room and the world seemed to go into slow-motion.

A cop, I don't remember his name, shouted from my room that something didn't add up. There were bloody, dried fingerprints on my window that didn't match, that couldn't match the dead inmate. They were much smaller, delicate – they belonged to *me*!

Chapter 20

In the days that followed Walter being found they were able to match his blood from my fingerprints, but it was still not adding up. There had to be *two* people who killed Walter, but I kept my mouth shut tight. I never thought she would say anything, but Laura announced it to the world like it was the second coming of Christ. She said that she '*loved*' me, and that she could produce the knives that killed Walter because she said, and I quote: *He was a man, and for that crime alone he deserved to die!* She said that it was a murder done for love, that we proved our love for each other by killing Walter. That and she wanted to hurt her mother, whom she said was no mother at all, she was just like an alley cat, always bringing trouble home with her.

She also told everyone what she had told Bill, the youth pastor from my church. She had announced that we were *in love*, and no amount of church would change that.

She never spoke of what happened to her baby's bones-I think that she buried them on the night of Walter's murder, so when I think of the old hallow I know there is a body buried in the ravine. I believe it was cathartic for Laura, that only she knows where his bones are laid.

Of course I denied it, the *love* part. As I said before, I kept my mouth shut about the murder. They had enough proof to convince the jury that I was insane, that's what my attorney had said, that I was caused to go insane by the murders of my sister and cousin. So the judge sentenced me between 25-30 years in a mental ward, just until I was not harmful to myself or others; that's a laugh, not harmful to myself or others? What does that even mean? *Not Heilstratten, of course-for the criminally insane* -no, now there are clean hospital settings, not *Heilstratten* at all; although they don't call them asylums as much these days.

240

Now they are called *psychiatric hospitals*. I guess I should count my blessings that I don't have to survive in the misery laden *Hell-stratten*. Am I crazy? I'm not even sure anymore, so many things have happened over this period of time; I'm not even sure anymore.

Laura was sentenced to life, in a hospital for the criminally insane, being it was a second time for her.

Marcus and *Rebecca. Yes, these are my friends, the only ones who dare keep me company.* Jolene married Mitch, and theirs was the only happy ending that came out of all this.

I still see Nancy and Margo in my sleep which causes my nightmares, or night terrors as they want to call them. I can smell the weedy plants from the lake, I smell the acrid way the train reeked as it burned and smoked the day of the accident. I see them cut up the way that Cromwell had left them. Even after all these years, they still bleed.

I keep on hearing Walter's voice in my sleep, telling me the diabolical things he had said about Nancy. I don't even believe the things he said about Margo. I don't believe it was true.

We all have choices to make throughout our entire lives, but then we have to be prepared to accept the consequences of our actions. I made some stupid choices mostly for believing in other people and not listening to my own conscience when it screamed and shouted I was wrong. Those choices have cost me my freedom, and I guess I deserve that. I should have tried harder to seek out the truth. Then, we all believe our own version of the truth, don't we?

www.ingramcontent.com/pod-product-compliance
Lightning Source LLC
Chambersburg PA
CBHW071302250626
47159CB00004B/1274